"Well, that was a pretty dirty trick." Libby rounded on Andreas. "Not telling me you were the new consultant."

"You didn't ask me. In fact you didn't even ask my name. You just passed out on me," he pointed out mildly, enjoying the blush that warmed her cheeks.

She stared at him incredulously. "Didn't you think that it might be embarrassing? Do you always mix business with pleasure?"

He gave a smile that was totally male. "That," he said slowly, "depends on the extent of the pleasure."

POSH DOCS

Dedicated, daring and devastatingly handsome—these doctors are guaranteed to raise your temperature!

Meet the doctors who are the best in the business....

Whether they're saving lives in the hospital, or romancing in the bedroom, they *always* get pulses racing!

THE GREEK CHILDREN'S DOCTOR

SARAH MORGAN

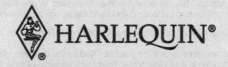

HARLEQUIN®

TORONTO • NEW YORK • LONDON
AMSTERDAM • PARIS • SYDNEY • HAMBURG
STOCKHOLM • ATHENS • TOKYO • MILAN • MADRID
PRAGUE • WARSAW • BUDAPEST • AUCKLAND

ISBN-13: 978-0-373-82046-7
ISBN-10:   0-373-82046-1

THE GREEK CHILDREN'S DOCTOR

First North American Publication 2004.

www.eHarlequin.com

Printed in U.S.A.

THE GREEK CHILDREN'S DOCTOR

CHAPTER ONE

'LIBBY, you're up for auction. Lot number 16.'

Libby snuggled the tiny baby in the crook of her arm and glanced up at the ward sister in horror. 'Tell me you're joking.'

'Deadly serious.' Beverley squinted down at the baby. 'How's she doing?'

'Better. I'm trying to get her to take more fluids,' Libby said softly, reaching for the bottle of milk that she'd warmed in readiness. 'And, Bev, I'm not taking part in the auction—I already told you that.'

'You have to!' The older woman sat down in the chair next to her and gave her a pleading look. 'You're the best-looking woman in the hospital. We're bound to get a good price for you.'

Libby pulled a face. 'That's so sexist!'

'But true.' Bev beamed at her. 'Come on. Say yes. It's for a good cause.'

'It's utterly degrading and I don't know what made you come up with the idea. You obviously have a sick mind.'

'It was *your* idea,' Bev reminded her placidly. 'But that was before you went off men again. Everyone's really entered into the spirit of things. It's going to be a great evening and we're going to raise a fortune for our playroom. This is going to be the best-equipped paediatric ward in the world.'

'Well, I must have been mad to think of it and I'm certainly not taking part. I'll give you a donation.' Libby gently placed the bottle to the baby's lips. 'Come on, sweetheart, suck for Libby.'

'That's not the same. It's not just about the money, it's

7

about team spirit and you have to be there. You're an important part of the paediatric team. My star performer, in fact.'

'In that case I'll come and watch.' Libby smiled with satisfaction as the baby clamped her mouth round the teat. 'There's a good girl.'

'We need you on that stage,' Bev said firmly, 'and just think of the opportunity to meet a new man! There'll be all sorts there. Short ones, tall ones, thin ones, fat ones...'

A new man?

Libby shuddered. 'It doesn't matter what they look like on the outside. They're all the same on the inside and I'm not interested.'

She'd given up on men totally. There was only so much hurt and disillusionment that a girl could stand.

Bev shifted uncomfortably. 'You have to. It's tomorrow night! They've printed the programmes and you're in it.'

'Oh, for crying out loud!' Libby glared at her colleague, who looked sheepish.

'It'll be fun,' she said lamely. 'A tall, handsome stranger will pay money for you. It's just a blind date really.'

'I don't do dates,' Libby said flatly, 'blind or otherwise.'

The way she felt at the moment, she had no intention of ever dating a man again.

'Well, you could do the choosing,' Bev suggested helpfully. 'It's not as if you're short of money. You could use some of that enormous trust fund that Daddy set up for you to purchase a really hot date.'

Libby shot her a look that spoke volumes. 'Do I look stupid?'

'Libby.' Bev spoke with exaggerated patience. 'You're twenty-nine years old and you're loaded. You shouldn't be single. At the very least, some man should be trying to marry you for your money.'

'Great. So now I'm up for sale to the highest bidder.' Libby looked at her friend in exasperation. 'What's wrong with being single? Women are allowed to be on their own these days. Being single is perfectly acceptable.'

'For some people, maybe,' Bev conceded, 'but not you. You adore children. Children adore you. You're cuddly and loving and fun. You were designed to be married and a mother.'

'The good thing about being a paediatric nurse,' Libby observed, 'is that you can enjoy the benefits of children without the drawbacks of a man.'

Bev sighed. 'Look, I know you haven't exactly had good experiences with men, but—'

'Good experiences?' Libby gave a laugh that was totally lacking in humour and then lowered her voice as the baby shifted restlessly in her arms. 'Bev, do I need to spell out just how utterly ridiculous I feel after what happened with Philip?'

Bev bit her lip. 'No. But you shouldn't feel ridiculous. You didn't do anything wrong.'

'I dated a married man,' Libby said shortly, and Bev frowned.

'But you didn't *know* he was married.'

'Not until I found him in bed with his wife,' Libby agreed. 'That sort of gave the game away really.'

Bev closed her eyes. 'I know you're hurt, but it wasn't your fault—'

'Of course it was. I was too trusting. He didn't mention a wife so I assumed he didn't have one. Silly me.' Libby struggled with a lump in her throat, cross with herself for becoming upset again. She'd promised herself that she wasn't going to waste another tear on Philip and here she was with a wobbly lip again. Pathetic! 'I am obviously totally incapable of spotting a rat so it's safer if I just stay single. So you can forget your auction. There's no way I'm ever voluntarily going on a date again.'

Bev cleared her throat delicately. 'You've got to have a

social life, Libby. What about the summer ball next month? You need a partner.'

'I'm not going to the summer ball.' Libby concentrated on the baby. 'I've decided to dedicate my life to work and forget about romance.'

Bev's eyes widened. 'You're not going to the ball? It's *the* event of the hospital calendar. If you don't go, Philip will assume that you're pining.'

'And if I do go, and he's there, then there'll be bloodshed,' Libby predicted darkly, adjusting the angle of the bottle slightly. 'He's a total rat. I've discovered that the better-looking the man, the higher the rat factor.'

Bev blinked. 'Rat factor?'

'Yes. It's my official measurement of male behaviour.'

Bev giggled. 'We shouldn't be having this conversation in front of the baby,' she murmured. 'She's only four months old. We'll shock her.'

'It's never too soon to learn about the rat factor,' Libby murmured. 'She'll have a head start on me. I was grown up before I discovered the truth.'

Actually, that wasn't strictly true, she reflected, watching as the baby guzzled the rest of the bottle. She'd had endless clues during her childhood.

'Men should come with a government health warning.'

'Not all men,' Bev said quietly, looking across the darkened ward at one of the fathers who sat slumped in a chair by a sleeping child. 'He's going to be with her for the rest of the night and he's going to have to do a full day's work tomorrow.'

'Yeah…' Libby followed her gaze. 'Dave is a saint. And Poppy is lucky to have such a devoted dad. But he's the exception. The rest of them are creeps.'

Poppy had cystic fibrosis and she'd developed yet another lung infection that required her to be back in hospital for treatment. She was well known on the ward and so was her father who never left her side.

Bev wasn't listening. 'If you wore something short and left your hair loose, you'd make us a fortune. If we hit our target it's going to mean a fantastic playroom for our children. Toys, desks, books by the million, a whiteboard for the teacher. It's just a bit of fun. *Please*, Libby…'

Libby opened her mouth to refuse again and then closed it with a resigned sigh.

It *had* been her idea so people would expect her to be there. But if she attended then she'd have to take part and she really, *really* didn't want to expose herself to an evening with a man.

Or give philandering Philip the opportunity to buy her and force the conversation she'd been avoiding.

Perhaps she could put such a high price on herself that no one would be able to afford her, she mused.

She continued to search for solutions as she eased the teat out of the baby's mouth and lifted her against her shoulder. The baby snuffled contentedly and Libby smiled, breathing in her warm baby smell and cuddling her closer. And suddenly the answer came to her. Her *brother* could buy her. Why hadn't she thought of it sooner?

'All right, I'll do it.' Libby smiled, pleased with her idea. 'Alex can buy me. At least that should ensure that no one else does.'

Especially Philip.

Ever since she'd arrived at Philip's flat unannounced and surprised him in a very compromising position with a stunning blonde who had turned out to be his wife—*a wife he'd never thought to mention*—Philip had been desperately trying to get to see her. He'd called her mobile so often that she'd finally switched it off and told her friends to call her on the ward. At least Bella, the receptionist, could field her calls.

She absolutely did not want a conversation with him about what had happened.

As far as she was concerned, there was nothing to talk about.

The man was married. And he'd lied to her.

'Did you manage to get any extra help for tomorrow?' She knew that the staffing situation was dire.

Bev shook her head gloomily. 'The nursing situation is bad, but fortunately the new consultant starts on Monday so at least we should finally have some more medical support.'

Libby nodded. They'd been a consultant short and that had put tremendous pressure on everyone.

'I'll come in early tomorrow,' she offered, and Bev bit her lip.

'I can't ask you to do that, you've worked a double shift today...'

'You didn't ask. I volunteered.'

Bev leaned forward and gave her a hug. 'You're brilliant, and if I were a man I'd definitely buy you.'

'And then you'd go home and sleep with a woman who turns out to be a wife that you conveniently forgot to mention,' Libby said dryly. 'So tell me—is the new consultant a woman or a rat?'

Bev laughed. 'He's a man, if that's what you're asking.'

'Oh well, you can't have everything.'

With a wistful smile Libby stroked the baby's smooth cheek and then laid her carefully back in her cot, tucking the sheet around her.

The baby was so beautiful. It made her terribly broody, caring for her, and she would have loved one of her own.

It was just a shame that having a baby required contact with a man.

Less than twenty-four hours later, Andreas Christakos strolled onto the ward, six feet three of broad-shouldered, drop-dead-handsome Greek male.

The night sister, confronted by this unexpected vision of

raw, masculine virility, dropped the pile of sheets she was carrying and lost her powers of speech.

Acknowledging that it probably hadn't been quite fair of him to arrive unannounced, Andreas extended a lean, bronzed hand and introduced himself.

The night sister paled slightly. 'You're the new consultant? We weren't exactly expecting you...' She stooped to pick up the sheets, visibly flustered by his unscheduled appearance. 'Did you want to see—? I mean, it seems a little late—'

'I merely came to familiarise myself with the whereabouts of the ward,' he assured her smoothly, his eyes flickering over the walls which were covered in brightly coloured children's paintings. 'I don't officially start until Monday.'

She clutched the sheets to her chest and looked relieved. 'That's what I thought. Good. Well, please, help yourself to the notes trolley—they're all there and any X-rays are underneath. We're pretty quiet for once, so everyone's slipped off to the auction,' the night sister told him. 'They'll be back when it finishes—or sooner if I call them.'

'*Auction?*' Andreas frowned as he repeated the word. He'd always thought his English was fluent but he found himself very unsure about what she was describing. Surely an auction involved paintings or other valuable artefacts?

'We're selling a date with each member of staff to raise money to buy equipment for our new playroom.'

Andreas, traditional and Greek to the very backbone, struggled with this concept. They were selling *dates*?

Aware that she was waiting for some sort of response, he dealt her a sizzling smile. 'It sounds like a novel way to raise money.'

'It is.' She looked at him for a moment and then smiled cheekily, her nervousness vanishing. 'You're very good-looking. Perhaps you should consider auctioning yourself.'

The smile froze on his face. 'I don't think so.'

He had enough trouble keeping women at a distance as

it was, and the one thing he absolutely didn't need was to offer himself to the highest bidder. The thought made him shudder. What sort of woman would that attract? Not the one he was searching for, that was for sure. Recent events had confirmed his growing suspicion that the woman he wanted didn't exist in real life.

'Are you sure I can't persuade you?' The night sister giggled. 'You'd make us a fortune! Well, just in case you change your mind, it's all happening in the doctors' bar in the basement. You could go and meet everyone. Half the hospital will be there. Introduce yourself. Buy yourself a date for the evening!'

Knowing that he had no intention of doing anything of the sort, Andreas merely smiled politely and reached for the first set of notes.

As he flicked to the first page, he reflected on the strange ways of the English. Like most of his countrymen, he was aware of the outlandish behaviour shown by some of the English girls who holidayed in Greece, but in all his time in various English hospitals he'd never come across a scenario where staff sold themselves to raise money.

Was the NHS really in that much trouble?

With a slight lift of his wide shoulders he dismissed the thought and proceeded to read the notes on each child, his sharp brain absorbing the information and filing it away for later.

An hour later he was thoroughly briefed on all the current admissions and he left the ward quietly, walking along the corridors that led to the main entrance, hesitating briefly as he reached the stairs that led down to the doctors' bar in the basement. Loud music drifted up the stairs, along with catcalls and much whooping and laughter.

Intrigued by the concept of anything so alien as an auction involving people, Andreas took the stairs and pushed open the door of the bar just as a leggy blonde sashayed down the improvised catwalk.

He stopped dead, his attention caught.

She was stunning.

Andreas sucked in a breath, his eyes raking over every inch of her slender, perfectly formed body. As he watched, she tossed her long, wavy blonde hair over her slim shoulders, her slanting blue eyes glinting as if she was daring someone to buy her.

She was wearing an almost indecently short pink dress and heels that were so high he feared for her safety, but she walked with a grace and elegance that was achingly feminine.

'Lot number 16.' The auctioneer laughed, raising his voice over the howls and wolf whistles. 'What am I bid for our Libby?'

There was a chorus of enthusiastic yells and the blonde rolled her eyes and grinned, striking an exaggerated pose that took his breath away.

Andreas surveyed her with unashamed lust, oblivious to the admiring glances he himself was drawing from the other females in the room.

Temporarily forgetting how jaded he was with women, he studied her closely and came to the conclusion that she was gorgeous. Physically. He didn't fool himself that her beauty went any deeper than that, but for a short-term relationship did that really matter? He wasn't inviting her to be the mother of his children so the intricacies of her personality were irrelevant.

'Ten pounds,' the auctioneer said. 'Let's start the bidding at £10.'

Andreas glanced at the auctioneer incredulously. Did the man have no idea of value?

'Yes.' A lanky blond man raised an arm and Andreas watched with interest as the girl's expression froze. All the warmth and humour drained out of her pretty face and she stared ahead stonily. It was clear to everyone watching that she didn't want to be purchased by the blond man.

She started moving again, and it was obvious from the way that her eyes slid frantically around the room that she was searching for someone. She seemed tense, almost desperate, and then her gaze rested on Andreas.

Startled eyes, as blue as the Aegean sea, widened and stared into his. Instead of continuing her rhythmic sway down the stage, she stopped dead, her whole body still, frozen by the connection that sizzled between them.

Taken aback by the strength of the attraction, Andreas felt his body tighten in that most primitive of male responses. His arrogant dark head angled back, he held her gaze, forgetting the recent change to his life that had fired his resolution to avoid women.

Suddenly all he wanted was her.

Naked. In his bed.

No self-respecting Greek male would allow a woman like her to pass by unscathed.

It would be a criminal waste.

Totally sure of himself, he strolled forward, indifferent to the lustful female stares he was attracting from all quarters. He was only interested in one woman and the confidence of his stride made the crowd part to let him through.

'One thousand pounds.' He delivered his bid coolly, his eyes still holding hers as he dropped the words into the expectant hush. He'd never paid for a woman in his life before, but there was no way he was letting the blond man buy her. Or any other man.

He wanted her for himself.

And Andreas Christakos was used to getting exactly what he wanted.

'One thousand pounds!' The auctioneer was almost incoherent with delight. 'Well, none of you tight individuals are going to top that so I'd say Libby's going, going, gone to the tall, dark stranger with the fat wallet!'

Ignoring the laughter, Andreas stretched out a lean, strong hand to Libby, his eyes still holding hers.

Looking slightly stunned, she stepped forward, descended the stage with care and took his hand, chin held high.

It was only when he caught her from falling at the bottom of the steps that he realised that she'd had too much to drink.

The blond man who'd bid £10 stepped forward, clearly desperate to speak to her, but she silenced him with an icy glare and Andreas felt her small hand tremble in his.

He frowned slightly. Why was she shaking?

In an instinctive male reaction, his hand tightened on hers possessively.

'No amount of money would induce me to have a conversation with you, Philip, let alone a date,' she said with exaggerated dignity. Having clarified the situation to her satisfaction, she turned to Andreas with a smile that would have illuminated Athens on a dark night. 'Shall we go?'

Andreas wondered what could have upset her so much that she'd be willing to leave the bar with a total stranger. She hadn't even asked his name and she was clinging to his hand as if it were a lifeline.

A totally inexplicable need to protect her slammed through him and he tightened his grip. 'Yes, let's go.'

He held the door open for her and she walked past him, long-legged and graceful, managing remarkably well on those high heels considering the volume of alcohol she appeared to have consumed. Up close she seemed more fragile than she had on the stage and he was suddenly aware of just how delicate she was compared to him. Her arms and wrists were slender, her waist was impossibly tiny and her long, slim legs seemed to go on for ever.

She climbed the stairs carefully, cheerfully greeting various members of the medical staff who passed. But he sensed that the cheerfulness was for everyone else's benefit and his firm mouth tightened as he contemplated the possible reasons for her distress. Obviously it had something to do with the blond man who thought she was only worth £10.

They reached the top of the stairs and he took her arm as they walked towards the car park.

'Exactly how much alcohol have you consumed?'

'None. I don't drink. Although perhaps I should have done tonight. At least alcohol might have numbed the utter humiliation of being on that stage. I can't believe I ever thought it would be a good idea. Thank goodness you came when you did. That creep almost bought me,' she slurred, bending down to remove her shoes. 'Ouch. Sorry. They're really uncomfortable.'

Did she think he was a fool?

It was perfectly obvious that she'd been drinking.

Andreas frowned. 'If you found it humiliating, why did you agree to do it?' he asked, noticing that without her shoes she had to tilt her head to look at him.

Her shoes dangled from her fingers. 'I did it because I promised that I would and I never break promises.'

'You didn't want to do it?'

'I would rather have dug a hole and buried myself,' she said frankly. 'Standing on that stage and trying to look cheerful was the hardest thing I've ever done in my life. I almost died with relief when you rescued me. For a horrible moment I thought that my rotten brother had abandoned me to my fate. Which reminds me, I need to write you a cheque.'

He looked at her blankly as she rummaged in her bag and produced a cheque book.

'A thousand pounds, wasn't it?' She scribbled on the cheque, tore it out and handed it to him. 'A bit steep, but never mind. It was very decent of you to turn up and buy me.'

She staggered slightly and Andreas closed both hands over her arms to steady her.

'Why are you giving me a cheque?'

She stared up at him vacantly and he found himself noticing the perfect shape of her mouth.

'Because that was the agreement.'

Still studying her mouth, Andreas struggled to concentrate. 'What agreement?'

She hesitated, obviously trying to retrieve something from her memory that the alcohol had wiped out. 'The agreement I made with my brother,' she said finally, a smile of triumph on her face as she remembered. 'He promised that if he couldn't make it he'd send someone else to save me from Philip, and…' she smiled at him dizzily '…he obviously sent you.'

Andreas dragged his eyes away from her mouth. 'I don't know your brother.'

She tilted her head and focused on him. 'You don't?' She bit her soft lip, confusion evident in her beautiful eyes. 'Alex promised me that if he was too busy to come he'd send someone to put in an outrageous bid for me so that no one else could buy me. I assumed it was you…'

He shook his head, totally intrigued. *Her brother had promised to buy her?* 'Not me.'

She swallowed hard. 'Well, if you didn't buy me for my brother then why did you—?' She broke off and backed away from him, her eyes suddenly wary. 'Who the hell are you? And why would you pay that much money for a stranger?'

'I thought that was the idea,' Andreas said mildly. Clearly she was questioning his motives and he could hardly blame her for that. 'Surely you wanted to persuade the audience to part with their money?'

'Well, yes, but not a *thousand pounds*.' She was still staring at him as if she expected him to attack her at any moment. 'If you think that paying all that money guarantees you—I mean, if you think that I'll…' She stumbled over the words, clearly embarrassed, and then gave up and gave him a threatening look. 'What I mean is, you're in for a serious disappointment because *I don't do that*!'

He hid his amusement. 'They were auctioning a *date*, Libby,' he reminded her calmly, and she glared at him.

'And doubtless you took that to mean sex because that's what all men expect, and then afterwards I discover the wife and the child.'

Andreas blinked, trying to keep up with her thought processes. 'I don't generally find I have to pay for sex,' he drawled, and she tipped her head on one side and studied him closely, her small pink tongue snaking out and moistening her lips.

'No, I'm sure you don't. But, then, I bet you don't usually have to pay for dates either.'

Andreas inclined his head. 'True.'

Normally he had to play all sorts of games to keep women at a distance.

Which made his current behaviour all the more unbelievable.

She obviously agreed with him if the expression on her face was anything to go by. 'So why did you pay such an outrageous amount of money for a date with *me*?'

He was asking himself the same question.

'Because I can afford it and because you're very beautiful,' he replied.

She took a few more steps backwards, clutching her shoes tightly. 'Well, I suggest you take the cheque I'm offering you,' she said coldly. 'I only agreed to do the auction because Alex promised he would buy me. I never, *ever* would have done it if I'd thought I'd actually have to go on a date. I don't date men. Men are rats and creeps.'

Andreas ran an experienced eye down a length of perfect thigh. A less likely candidate for celibacy he had yet to see. But there was no missing the utter misery in her blue eyes.

It didn't take a genius to work out that someone had obviously hurt her badly.

'You've obviously been mixing with the wrong men,' he said softly, and she gave a humourless laugh.

'Funnily enough, I've worked that out for myself. From now on, no more relationships.'

Unable to resist teasing her, Andreas smiled. 'What about sex?'

He watched with fascination as colour bloomed in her cheeks.

'I'm old-fashioned,' she muttered. 'I don't have sex without a relationship and seeing that men are hopeless at relationships, I've given up.'

'So tell me.' He stepped closer to her, his attention caught by the fullness of her lower lip. 'Who was responsible for putting you off relationships?'

'You want the short version or the long version?' She shrugged carelessly but he guessed that she was battling with tears and he frowned, wondering what it was about her that made him feel so protective. Not that she would have thanked him for those feelings, he reflected wryly. These days women wanted to hunt their own dragons and kill them.

'Whichever you want to tell me.'

'Well, I suppose I'd have to start with my parents, who were definitely *not* a shining example of marital harmony. They never touched.' She flashed him a suggestive smile. 'Well, of course, they must have touched *once*, or they wouldn't have had me, but fortunately for them they had triplets so they managed to get all the physical contact out of the way in one go.'

Andreas thought of his own childhood and the love and emotional support he'd been given. It had been something that he'd taken for granted at the time, but his work as a paediatrician had brought him into contact with enough children from less privileged backgrounds than his for him to have been able to appreciate the impact that parental disharmony could have on a child's view of life.

'Their relationship put you off men?'

'That and personal experience in the field,' she said

gloomily. 'My most recent disaster turned out to be married.'

Andreas frowned. 'That's what you meant by your comment about discovering the wife and child? You've definitely been dating the wrong men.'

'Don't use that smooth, seductive tone on me,' she advised, swaying slightly as she looked at him. 'It is totally wasted. I don't trust *anyone*. From now on I'm cynical and suspicious. And the more attractive the man, the higher my index of suspicion. I ought to warn you that with you it's soaring through the roof.'

Before he could reply he saw her glance over his shoulder and her whole body tensed.

Wondering what had caused her reaction, he turned his head briefly and saw the blond man hurrying towards them, looking agitated.

'Oh, help—here he comes again. What does it take to get him to leave me alone?' She lifted her chin bravely but he saw the anguish in her blue eyes.

Andreas knew exactly how to persuade the man to leave her alone.

Telling himself that he was merely helping a damsel in distress, he pulled her firmly against him and lowered his mouth to hers.

He felt her stiffen in surprise and then melt against him, her mouth opening under the subtle pressure of his. She was all feminine temptation, her floral scent wrapping itself around him and drawing him in, her lips all sweetness and seduction as she kissed him back.

Andreas was taken aback by the strength of his reaction to that kiss. His body throbbed with instant arousal and he cupped her face with confident hands, feeling her quiver of surprise as he deepened the kiss. She dropped the shoes she was holding and clutched at his shirt, whimpering slightly under the skilled assault of his mouth.

Stunned by her uninhibited response and his own powerful reaction, he hauled her closer still and stroked a leisurely hand up her thigh, the warmth of her smooth skin intensifying the throbbing, pulsing ache of his erection.

Feeling fireworks explode in his head, Andreas continued to explore her mouth, building the excitement to such dangerous levels that it threatened to engulf them both.

It was the hottest, most erotic kiss he'd ever experienced and it wouldn't have ended there if it hadn't been for the loud slam of a car door that jerked them both back to the reality of their surroundings.

Andreas lifted his head, considerably shaken by his definitely uncharacteristic response to the woman who now stood quivering in his arms.

He glanced around him in utter disbelief, taking in the ordered rows of cars interspersed by the odd streetlamp. He'd always prided himself in his self-control and yet here he was ready to slam this woman against the nearest convenient surface and make love to her hard and fast until she begged for mercy.

What the hell had happened to him?

Not only were they in a public place but he was also aware that, whatever she said to the contrary, she'd had too much to drink and was obviously on the rebound.

Neither factors provided a good basis for any sort of relationship.

Cursing softly in Greek, he released her and then caught her again as she stumbled.

She looked at him, bemused. 'Feel dizzy,' she muttered, her expression dazed and disconnected, her blue eyes cloudy as she lifted a finger to her lips.

He felt pretty dizzy himself.

Remembering just how good it had felt, Andreas fought the temptation to kiss her again. There would be other occasions, he reminded himself, and next time he was going to select the venue more carefully and ban alcohol. She looked as though she was about to collapse in a heap.

'I'd better take you home.'

Before he committed an indecent act in a public place.

And when she was sober he'd arrange a proper date in a place where there'd be absolutely no chance of interruptions.

He stooped to pick up the shoes she'd dropped and then pointed his key towards his car and unlocked it. Suddenly aware that she was swaying again, he swept her off her feet and carried her to his car, trying to ignore her feminine scent and the way her soft hair tickled his cheek.

'Put me down.' Her words were slightly slurred and she wriggled in his arms. 'I hate men. I don't want to go on a date. And I don't want another kiss. It made me feel strange.'

Her head flopped back and he deposited her in the passenger seat, trying valiantly to ignore the fact that her dress had ridden up and was now revealing every perfect inch of her long legs. Her eyes closed and Andreas stared at her in exasperation.

'What exactly did you drink tonight?'

'One glass of really, *really* delicious orange juice,' she murmured sleepily, and he rolled his eyes.

Did she really expect him to believe that?

She was barely coherent!

'I need to take you home,' he drawled, wondering if she knew just how big a risk she was taking by getting so drunk that she didn't know who she was with. She hadn't even asked his name.

'Give me your address.' He slammed the driver's door shut and turned to look at her, groaning with frustration as he saw her curled up in his passenger seat as snug and comfortable as a tiny kitten. She was fast asleep.

His patience severely tested, Andreas sat back in his seat and counted to ten while he contemplated the problem.

So much for taking her home.

He had absolutely no intention of going back to the bar

to discover her address, so he really had no option other than to take her back to his house. Which made life extremely complicated because Adrienne was there.

He closed his eyes briefly and swore under his breath.

The evening was definitely not ending the way he'd intended.

CHAPTER TWO

LIBBY awoke with a crushing headache.

With a whimper of self-pity she sat up and found herself looking into a pair of curious brown eyes. A girl sat on the end of her bed. Underneath the unruly brown hair and layers of make-up, Libby guessed her to be about twelve.

'Wow.' The girl studied her closely. 'You look *really* ill.'

Libby bit back a groan and closed her eyes. She had absolutely no idea where she was but she knew she had an almighty hangover.

Which didn't really make sense because she hadn't touched alcohol.

Or, at least, not intentionally.

Suspicion entering her mind she lifted a hand to her aching skull and sat up slowly, wincing slightly as a shaft of sunlight probed through the curtain and stabbed her between the eyes.

Realising that she was lying in an enormous, elegant bedroom, panic swamped her.

Whose bedroom?

Just what had happened last night?

The girl was still studying her closely, as if she couldn't understand how anyone could look so awful and still be alive. '*Yiayia* made Andreas promise that he'd never bring a woman home while I was in the house, so I suppose that means he's in love with you.'

What?

Who was the girl sitting on the bed?

And who the hell was Andreas?

Searching her aching brain for some recollection of what had happened the night before, Libby had a sudden memory

26

of broad, muscular shoulders, a firm mouth and lots and lots of fireworks.

Yes, there'd definitely been fireworks.

'I…er…who exactly is *Yiayia*?'

'*Yiayia* is Greek for Grandma, and you've said enough, Adrienne.' Cool male tones came from the doorway and the girl scrambled off the bed, suddenly wary.

'There's no need to use that scary tone. I'm old enough to know the facts of life and I know all about sex.' She looked at Libby curiously. 'Did you have sex? *Yiayia* says that loads of women want to go to bed with Andreas because he's seriously rich and very good-looking. Women go mad about him.'

Deprived of her powers of speech, Libby glanced helplessly at the man in the doorway and clashed with the darkest, sexiest eyes she'd ever seen. Despite her somewhat pathetic state, her mouth fell open and she did something she never did when she met a man.

She *stared*.

He was well over six feet, powerfully built, with jet black hair smoothed back from his forehead and bronzed skin that suggested a Mediterranean heritage. He possessed all the arrogant self-assurance of a man who'd been chased by women from the cradle.

She felt herself colour under his sharp gaze. It was evident from the hint of mockery in his dark eyes that he realised that she had an extremely hazy recollection of the events of the night before.

'You talk too much, Adrienne.' Without shifting his gaze from Libby's pale face, he strolled into the bedroom and she noticed for the first time that he was carrying a mug. 'Drink that.' He placed a mug of black coffee on the bedside table. 'It will help.'

Confronted by this final confirmation that he was well aware of her delicate condition, Libby shrank back against the pillow, stricken with guilt at her own behaviour.

She'd obviously been horribly drunk the night before.
What she didn't understand was *how*.

Unlike her, he was fully dressed and she was uncomfortably aware of his wide shoulders and sleek, dark good looks next to her near nakedness. Deciding that so much masculine virility was too much for a woman with a headache, Libby reached for the coffee.

Grandma had a point, she thought weakly. She didn't know about the rich bit, but he was *incredibly* good-looking. Almost enough to make a woman forget that all men were rats.

Which was evidently what she must have done when she'd agreed to go back to his flat with him.

How could she have done such a thing?

She never took risks like that!

She was obviously seriously on the rebound.

Catching sight of her pink dress draped carelessly over the back of a chair, she gave a whimper of mortification.

How had it got there? She had absolutely no recollection of getting undressed. Realising that she was wearing a white silk shirt that she'd never seen before in her life, her stomach flipped.

What exactly *had* happened the night before?

She remembered arriving at the auction and being given a drink of orange juice by Bev.

And she *definitely* remembered fireworks.

'*Yiayia* says that if a man and a woman spend a night together they *have* to get married,' the girl said firmly, and the man said something sharp in a language that Libby assumed was Greek before switching to English.

'Go and get ready for school,' he ordered, 'and wash that muck off your face. They'll refuse to have you back if you look like that.'

'That's why I did it,' the girl said moodily, and he sighed, the long-suffering sigh of a man stretched to the limits of his patience.

'You know you have to go back.' His voice was firm but held a note of sympathy. 'Just until we sort this out. I'm interviewing housekeepers next week.'

Adrienne looked at him. 'If you got married you wouldn't need to employ a housekeeper. It's time you settled down with a decent woman, not someone like—'

'Adrienne!' This time the man's voice was icy cold. 'That's enough. Go and wash your face.'

The girl's slim shoulders sagged. 'But—'

'Now!'

The commanding tone evidently worked because Adrienne subsided and left the room with a last curious look at Libby.

There was a long silence and Libby felt her colour rise.

Feeling that someone ought to say something, she put her coffee down and pushed her tangled blonde curls out of her eyes. 'Er…about last night…'

Not having a clue what had actually taken place the previous night, she left the statement hanging, hoping that he'd be enough of a gentleman to say something reassuring, but he merely looked at her quizzically and waited for her to finish.

Libby sighed. He was obviously one of those enviable people who used silence as a weapon, whereas she, unfortunately, had never mastered the art.

'Look.' Deciding that directness was the best approach, she took a deep breath. 'Did you spike my drink last night?'

He lifted a dark eyebrow. 'You think I need to render a woman senseless in order to persuade her to come home with me?'

No, she didn't think that.

He was the embodiment of most women's fantasies.

She flushed and concluded from his amused expression that he obviously wasn't the one responsible for her pounding headache.

'I'm sorry, it's just that someone must have but I really

don't remember that much—except the fireworks. They were great. What did—?' She broke off and cleared her throat nervously. 'Well, obviously you brought me back here, which was very kind of you, but did we—? I mean, I don't remember if we actually— You see, I don't do that sort of thing usually, but I suppose I must have been a bit upset last night and…'

Totally disconcerted by his continued silence, she gave a groan and hid her head under the covers.

Why didn't he say something?

And what exactly had they done?

She was never, *ever* going out again.

It was just too embarrassing.

Finally she felt the bed shift under his weight and the covers were firmly pulled away from her.

'Two things,' he said softly, and she decided that although he didn't say much, it was definitely worth the wait when he did. He spoke with a slight accent, his deep voice caressing her nerve endings and soothing her aching head. The tension oozed out of her and she felt herself relax. His voice was amazing. 'Firstly, you should know that when I make love to a woman, Libby, she *always* remembers it.'

The tension was back with a vengeance. Her breath trapped in her lungs, heart thudding against her rib cage, Libby swallowed hard and stared into his very amused eyes.

He exuded a raw, animal sex appeal that took her breath away and she felt a powerful urge to slide her arms round his strong neck and kiss him.

She could well imagine that a night with him would be an unforgettable experience.

Appalled by the uncharacteristically explicit nature of her own thoughts, she pulled her mind back to the present and tightened her grip on the covers as if they could afford her some protection.

'Right.' Her voice was little more than a squeak. 'And what was the second thing?'

'The second thing is that there *were* no fireworks…' he dealt her a sizzling smile that sent an electric current through her trembling body '…until I kissed you.'

And with that he stood up and left the room, closing the door firmly behind him.

Having dropped Adrienne at her boarding school, Andreas strolled onto the ward an hour later, immediately aware of the consternation his appearance created.

Having recognised him from the night before, the staff were all evidently wondering what had happened to Libby.

'*You're* the new consultant?' The ward sister stared at him and then gave him a weak smile. 'Er, I'm Bev—and you're a day early.'

Andreas lifted a broad shoulder. 'I like to be on top of things.'

Bev bit her lip. 'We noticed you last night. But we didn't know—I mean, we didn't recognise you.'

'Of course you didn't.' He'd been careful not to introduce himself to anyone.

Bev took a deep breath and asked the question that she was obviously dying to ask. 'What did you do with Libby?'

Not what he'd wanted to do.

'I left her to sleep it off,' he drawled, moving to the notes trolley. 'Do the nurses on this ward always party that hard?'

Bev's shoulders stiffened defensively. 'For your information, we're desperately short-staffed and Libby worked sixteen hours on the trot yesterday and the same the day before. She had no breaks and nothing to eat all day. It's not surprising she was tipsy.'

Andreas refrained from pointing out that she'd been more than tipsy. By the time he'd laid her on the bed and undressed her, she'd been unconscious.

But she seemed to be under the impression that she hadn't drunk anything.

'Well, I have to warn you not to expect her in today,' he

said smoothly. He remembered how pale and exhausted she'd looked when he'd left her, her amazing blonde hair spread over the pillow in his spare bedroom.

Mindful of Adrienne's presence, he'd resisted the temptation to join her on the bed and apply his considerable skills to bringing some colour to her cheeks.

'She's not due in until later anyway, and Libby's got the stamina of an ox. She'll be here.' Bev grabbed a set of notes and smiled at him hopefully. 'As you're early, I don't suppose you'd see a child for me, would you? The rest of your team all seem to be tied up elsewhere and I think her drain could probably come out.'

Andreas held out his hand for the notes. 'Let's go.'

Libby arrived on the ward later that morning, changed into the bright blue tracksuit bottoms and red T-shirt that all the nurses wore when they were on duty and tied her hair back with a matching ribbon.

The black coffee had helped enormously. Her head was still pounding but it was as much from tiredness as anything else. She'd worked so many double shifts in the last month that she'd forgotten what the inside of her own flat looked like.

And after last night…

She groaned at the memory, stuffed the white shirt and the pink dress into her locker and went in search of Bev.

She found her by the drugs trolley.

'*What* did you put in that orange juice?' Libby glanced over her shoulder to check that no one was listening. 'Someone spiked my drink and I've just worked out that it had to have been you.'

'Vodka,' Bev muttered, not quite meeting her eyes.

Libby stared at her, appalled. '*Vodka?* For crying out loud, Bev! I hadn't had a single thing to eat all day. What were you doing?'

'Giving you courage,' Bev said calmly, her eyes still on the drugs trolley. 'You were nervous.'

'*Nervous?* Thanks to you, I could hardly walk!'

'You looked fine. Better than fine. Really relaxed and sexy. We got £1000 for you. That cheque boosted our funds no end. Do you know how much we made?'

'I don't care how much we made.' Libby groaned and covered her face with her hands. 'Do you realise that I woke up in a strange bed this morning, in the house of a strange man who I don't even remember?' Her hands dropped to her sides and she frowned at Bev. 'What's the matter with you? Why aren't you looking at me?'

Bev looked hideously uncomfortable and Libby felt a sinking feeling in the pit of her stomach.

'There's more, isn't there?'

The ward sister tensed awkwardly. 'Well, there is something I probably ought to tell you—and you're not going to be pleased. It's about the man who bought you last night. Actually, he's—'

Loud screams interrupted her and Libby winced and glanced towards the ward. '*Who* is *that*?'

'Little Marcus Green.' Bev pulled a face. 'He had his hernia repair and his mother's had to leave him to sort out a crisis at home. Not a happy child.'

The screaming intensified and Libby rubbed her aching head. 'Poor little mite. I'll go and see to him,' she muttered. 'We'll finish this conversation later.'

'No!' Bev grabbed her arm. 'Libby, wait, I really need to tell you about the man who bought you. He's—'

'Later.' Libby shrugged her off and walked off down the ward, ponytail swinging as she hurried towards the sound.

One of the staff nurses was trying to distract him and she gave a sigh of relief when she saw Libby. 'I'm glad to see you. He's been like this for hours. His mum had to go and see to the older one at home and he's been hysterical ever since.'

Libby scooped the screaming toddler into her arms, careful not to damage the wound, and carried him over to the pile of colourful cushions that were piled in the corner of the ward.

'There, sweetheart. You'll soon feel better.' She dropped a kiss on top of his head. 'Shall we have a story while we wait for Mummy? I know you love stories.'

Marcus continued to sob and hiccough and Libby cuddled him close as she selected a book and settled down on the cushions with the little boy on her lap. 'You can choose. "Three Little Pigs" or "Little Red Riding Hood"?'

The toddler's sobs lessened. 'Pigs.'

'Three Little Pigs it is, then,' Libby said, reaching for the book and giving a gasp. 'Oh, my goodness, have you seen this?'

At her excited tone the toddler stopped sobbing and stared.

'What a cute piggy,' Libby said happily, and Marcus sneaked his thumb into his mouth and snuggled onto her lap for a closer look.

'Once upon a time...' Libby spoke in a soft voice and several other children slid out of their beds and joined her on the cushions, all listening round-eyed as she told the story.

Having examined the baby and given instructions for the drain to be removed, Andreas walked back through the ward and stopped dead at the sight of Libby, her blonde hair caught back in a bright ribbon, almost buried under a group of contented children.

They were snuggled close to her, listening avidly as she read, one of them holding onto her hand and another settled comfortably on her lap.

She was a little pale, but apart from that she looked none the worse for her excesses of the night before.

In fact, she looked incredibly beautiful and desire slammed through him again.

Bev appeared by his side. 'I told you she'd be here,' she said airily, and relieved him of the notes. 'Don't disturb her now. That toddler has been screaming since he woke up. We were all at our wits' end. We've given him painkillers but they didn't help. He needed comfort and that's Libby's speciality.'

Was it?

Andreas stared, his attention held by Libby who was laughing at something one of the children had said. She was gentle and smiley and thoroughly at home with the children. Frankly, it wasn't what he'd expected. Having seen her on the stage, he'd expected shallow and frivolous and what he was seeing was something completely different.

He watched, feeling something shift inside him. After his recent experiences, he'd given up on meeting a woman who found children anything other than a nuisance.

'She's good with them.' His soft observation drew Bev's glance.

'Yeah, she's better than most drugs. No one cheers the children up like Libby,' she told him. 'She's the best. This ward would have collapsed without her. She does the work of three.'

As they watched, the little boy snuggled closer and Libby curved an arm around him and cuddled him closer.

She was a natural storyteller, her eyes twinkling with enthusiasm and mischief as she emphasised the drama and held their attention.

She'd just got to the part where the wolf fell into the hot water when she looked up and saw him, her eyes widening with recognition. Her gaze slid to Bev in silent question and her cheeks turned pink with mortification as understanding dawned.

Bev gave a weak smile and shrugged helplessly.

'More.' The toddler tugged her arm, frustrated that the

story had stopped and oblivious to the drama being played out around him. 'Want more story.'

Libby swallowed, obediently croaked her way to the end and then scrambled to her feet, Marcus still in her arms.

Bev cleared her throat. 'This is Andreas Christakos, the new consultant.' She spoke in a bright, professional voice that did nothing to alleviate the tension in the air. 'Andreas, this is Elizabeth Westerling. We call her Libby. I think you've already met each other...' Her voice trailed off slightly, and Libby closed her eyes briefly, her cheeks still pink with embarrassment.

One of the little girls tugged at her clothes. 'I need the toilet, Libby.'

'I'll take you, sweetheart,' Bev said quickly, catching her by the hand, obviously eager to find an excuse to get away.

Another little boy stepped closer. 'Is that the end of the story?'

Dragging her gaze away from his, Libby glanced down and managed a smile. 'For now. I've got to do some work.'

'Can we have another story later?'

'Maybe. If there's time.' She stroked Marcus's hair and put him back in his cot. She looked pale from lack of sleep and there were dark rings under her eyes but her beauty still took Andreas's breath away.

There were sparks of accusation in her eyes as she turned to face him. 'Well, that was a pretty dirty trick.'

He lifted an eyebrow quizzically and she glared at him coldly.

'Not telling me you were the new consultant.'

'You didn't ask me. In fact, you didn't even ask my name. You just passed out on me,' he pointed out mildly, enjoying the blush that warmed her cheeks. She had incredible skin. Smooth and creamy and untouched by the harshness of the sun.

'But *you* knew who I was,' she said accusingly. 'You knew I worked on the ward.'

'There was a strong chance of it.' He lifted a broad shoulder. 'So?'

She stared at him incredulously. 'Didn't you think that it might be embarrassing? Do you always mix business with pleasure?'

He gave a smile that was totally male. 'That,' he said slowly, 'depends on the extent of the pleasure.'

'Right.' She stared at him for a long moment and then looked away, her chest rising and falling rapidly. 'Well, at least I can save myself postage. Your shirt is in my locker.'

'My shirt?'

'The shirt you dressed me in, *Dr Christakos*.' Her voice was loaded with accusation. 'When I was asleep. Remember?'

Of course he remembered.

He remembered every delectable inch of her. 'I didn't think you'd be very comfortable sleeping in that pink thing. It seemed a little tight.'

'Excuse me?' She arched an eyebrow. 'I'm supposed to be *grateful* that you undressed me?'

'Calm down,' he drawled, his eyes gleaming with amusement. 'I kept my eyes closed the whole time. Well—most of the time.'

Libby's mouth tightened and she grabbed his arm and dragged him into the treatment room.

'I think we'd better get a few things straight.' Her blue eyes flashed at him as she let the doors swing closed behind her. 'I only allowed you to buy me because I thought my brother had sent you. I had no intention of going on a date with anyone.'

'You're angry because I bought you?' He lifted an eyebrow. 'You would have preferred me to have stood aside and let the blond man buy you?'

She stiffened slightly. 'No, of course not.'

'I seem to remember you holding onto me pretty tightly last night.'

His dark eyes glittered with amusement and she coloured. 'Yes, well, at the time I thought you were rescuing me.'

'I was.'

She glanced at him impatiently. 'You know what I mean! I thought my brother had sent you.'

He shrugged carelessly. 'He didn't, but I don't see the problem.'

'There is no problem, providing you take the £1000 back,' she said, and he smiled.

'I don't want the money,' he said smoothly. 'I paid for a date and that's what I want.'

And this time he was going to take the kiss to its natural conclusion.

She lifted her chin. 'And do you always get what you want?'

He smiled. 'Always.'

She sucked in a breath, looking slightly taken aback. 'Well, you won't on this occasion. I don't date men.'

Andreas leaned broad shoulders against the wall and tried to adjust to the fact that he'd just been turned down by a woman. It was a totally new experience.

'So...' He shrugged casually. 'You get to know me a little, and then you say yes.'

Her mouth fell open. 'Confident, aren't you?'

'Remember the fireworks, Libby.'

She stilled and her eyes connected with his. For a long moment she stared at him and then she swallowed and backed away, hoping that distance would cure the fluttering in her stomach. 'Leave me alone. I'm very grateful that you rescued me from Philip last night and I'm grateful that you took me home when I was in a less than coherent state—'

'You were drunk,' he slotted in helpfully, and she winced.

'I hadn't eaten anything all day and I had one vodka— apparently.' She rubbed slim fingers across her temple as if the memory alone was enough to inflict a headache. 'It was hidden in the orange juice.'

Hidden?

'Anyway.' She looked at him warily. 'It's history now.'

His gaze slid down her slim body, noting that she was trembling and that her hands were clenched into fists by her sides.

Despite her protests, it was blindingly obvious that she was as strongly affected by their encounter as he'd been, and it was hardly surprising. The chemistry between them was overwhelmingly powerful.

Gratified and encouraged by her response to him, he folded his arms across his broad chest and reminded himself that she'd been badly hurt. It was just a question of patience. 'It isn't history. You owe me a date.'

'Haven't you learned the meaning of the word "no"? What the hell is the matter with you men?' She glared at him with frustration and then stalked across the treatment room, pausing to look at him as she reached the door. 'In case you've forgotten, you have a little girl at home. I don't think your wife would be too impressed if she could hear you now.'

Andreas tensed, reflecting on how close he'd come to being in exactly the position she'd described.

If it hadn't been for Adrienne he'd have made a colossal mistake.

'I don't have a wife,' he said softly, 'and Adrienne isn't my daughter, she's my niece. But it's true that I do have a responsibility towards her for the time being, which is why you slept in the spare room last night and not in my bed.'

Colour flared in her cheeks and she sucked in a breath. 'I would not have been in your bed, Dr Christakos. I don't do things like that.'

'You didn't know whose bed you were in,' he pointed out, touching her flushed cheek with a strong finger. 'That might be a point worth remembering next time you have a drink.'

'Perhaps you should address your comments to the ward sister,' she muttered, and he frowned.

So it was the ward sister who'd spiked her drink. Which explained why she'd been so worried about Libby when he'd walked onto the ward alone.

Well, next time he took Libby out he was going to make sure that she didn't touch a drop of alcohol. He wanted her stone cold sober.

'What time are you off duty?'

'That is none of your business. What was it your niece said? That women are always chasing you for your looks and your money?' She tilted her head to one side. 'I don't normally tell people this on such a short acquaintance, but it's probably only fair to warn you that my father is one of the richest men in England and I've always been hideously suspicious of really good-looking men. So you have absolutely nothing to offer me.'

'How about fireworks?' He stepped closer to her, amused by the way she snatched in her breath and glared at him. She was trying so hard to pretend that she wasn't interested in him and he found it surprisingly endearing.

'Remember those fireworks, Libby,' he drawled softly, lifting a hand and trailing a finger down the slim line of her throat. 'Next time we're going to set them off in private.'

She stared at him like a rabbit caught in headlights. 'There won't be a next time and I won't be seeing you in private. I'm not interested.'

Her anguished rejection of their attraction made his heart twist. It was like dealing with an injured animal.

'I paid for a date with you, Libby,' he reminded her calmly, 'and I intend to claim it.'

Deciding that the first step in her rehabilitation was to kiss her when she was sober, he slid both hands around her face and tilted it, his eyes dropping to her mouth as her lips parted and she sucked in a breath.

Underneath his fingers he could feel a pulse beating in

her throat and he lowered his head slowly, deliberately, closing the gap between them.

Her blue eyes locked with his, their breath mingling, and when their mouths finally touched he gave a groan of satisfaction, his tongue tracing the seam of her lips in a sensual onslaught that left her shivering.

He kissed her slowly and thoroughly and when he finally lifted his head she just stared at him, visibly shocked, and he couldn't prevent the smile of all-male satisfaction that tugged at his mouth.

'Now try telling me you're not interested, Libby.'

Without giving her a chance to recover and deliver a suitable response, he left the treatment room and went back to work, deciding that his new job was looking better all the time.

Libby stood frozen to the spot in the treatment room, her whole body trembling.

Her head had been full of a thousand things that she'd wanted to say, and they'd all vanished the moment his mouth had met hers.

She'd never been particularly into kissing if she was honest. Her mind usually wandered and she found herself inventing excuses to end the evening promptly.

But now she realised that she'd never really been kissed before.

Not properly.

Andreas Christakos had kissed her properly. His kiss had been a full-blown seduction which had affected her ability to think coherently.

In fact, the way he kissed made her feel *so* hot and he made her want *more*.

If that was the starter then she definitely wanted the main course.

Libby gave a horrified groan and covered her face with her hands.

And the worst thing was that he knew it.

He'd kissed her into a state of quivering, shameless excitement and had then strolled casually out of the room with all the arrogant self-confidence of a man who didn't know the meaning of rejection.

Libby's hands dropped to her sides and she tried to pull herself together.

No more kissing, she vowed silently. Absolutely no more kissing. It turned her brain to mush and there was no way she was going to be able to keep him at a safe distance if he did it again.

He was *so* good-looking it was hard to concentrate and it would have been very, very easy to give in to all that Greek charm.

But she wasn't going to.

And she definitely wasn't going on a date with him.

He'd be the same as all the others. Worse probably, if his niece was to be believed. What had she said? That women were always chasing after him?

Libby shuddered. Those sorts of men were always the worst. Smug and arrogant. And definitely not to be trusted.

If he expected her to do any chasing then he was in for a shock. She had more sense than to fall for a pair of sexy dark eyes and an incredible body.

She was going to be running as hard as she could in the opposite direction, and now she knew where to find him she'd be delivering him a cheque at the first opportunity.

She lifted her hand to her mouth, touching her lips gently, wondering whether it was obvious to everyone that she'd just been kissed. She felt as though it was branded on her forehead.

Taking a deep breath, she pushed open the door of the treatment room, glancing furtively around her to check that no one was watching.

She could do it, she told herself firmly. She was a professional and she could work with this man.

OK, so he obviously had a Ph.D. in kissing and he was

totally different from doctors that she worked with on a daily basis, but she could do it.

Bev sidled up to her, looking sheepish. 'Er, Libby…'

Libby glared at her. This was all her fault! 'Go away. You are *not* my favourite person right now.'

'Libby, the man's gorgeous, you should be thanking me for making it happen.'

'*Thanking you?*' Libby let out a choked laugh. 'Thanks to you, our new consultant thinks I'm a dizzy, brainless lush with a sad love life.'

'He paid £1000 for one date with you,' Bev pointed out wistfully. 'That's an enormous sum of money. He can't think you're that bad.'

Libby groaned and rubbed slim fingers over her aching forehead. 'I can't believe you got me into this mess. How am I *ever* going to have any credibility with him?'

'You're a great nurse,' Bev said firmly. 'The minute he sees you in action, he'll be bowled over.'

'He undressed me,' Libby hissed in an outraged tone, and Bev's eyes widened.

'Wow. You lucky thing.'

Libby looked at her blankly. 'Lucky?'

'Libby, he's *gorgeous*,' Bev breathed wistfully. 'He is the most stunning-looking man I've ever laid eyes on.'

'Precisely. His rat factor must be off the scale.'

Bev rolled her eyes. 'If someone fancied me enough to pay £1000 for a date, then as far as I'm concerned they could have me for ever. It's incredibly romantic.'

'It's not romantic. It's embarrassing. And, thanks to you, from now on I'm going to have to avoid him. And how am I going to work with a man I have to avoid? *Aargh!*' Libby rolled her eyes in frustration and at that moment one of the more junior nurses hurried up.

'Libby, can you take a look at Rachel Miller for me, please? The GP sent her in an hour ago with a very high temperature and it's showing no sign of coming down. I don't like the look of her. She's still waiting to be seen by one of the doctors but they've been caught up in clinic and I wasn't sure whether to bother the new consultant.'

With a last meaningful look at Bev, Libby followed her colleague down the ward and into one of the side rooms that had cots and beds for parents who wanted to stay.

The baby was in a side ward and Libby could see instantly that she was very poorly. She lay still in the cot, her breathing noisy and her cheeks flushed. Immediately Libby snapped into professional mode, her personal worries forgotten.

The baby's mother was by her side, pale and worried. 'She's really floppy and so, so hot.'

'Can you tell me what happened?' Libby spoke softly, her eyes fixed on the child, assessing her breathing. 'When did she become ill?'

'She was a bit under the weather yesterday morning and then she just got worse and worse. By teatime she was just lying on the sofa.'

And she was just lying now. Totally unresponsive. It wasn't a good sign.

'Could you get her interested in anything—toys, books?'

The mother shook her head. 'Nothing. She just lay there. Finally I panicked and took her to the GP and he sent us in here.'

'And when did she last have paracetamol syrup?'

'Two hours ago.' The mother looked at her anxiously. 'What's going to happen?'

'I'm going to check her temperature now and then ask one of the doctors to see her straight away.' Libby reached for the thermometer. 'Has she had all her immunisations, Mrs Miller?'

'Please, call me Alison and, yes, she's had everything.'

'Good.'

Libby checked the temperature and recorded it on the

chart. 'It's very high, as you know. Has she been drinking much?'

'She's just not interested in anything.'

'When did she last have a wet nappy?'

The mother looked startled by the question. 'I don't know…'

'It's a way of judging her fluid output,' Libby explained, and the woman nodded.

'Oh, I see.' She frowned slightly. 'I suppose I changed it about three hours ago.'

Libby checked the child's blood pressure and then gave Alison Miller a brief smile.

'OK, well, the next thing to do is to ask one of our doctors to see her. We need to find out what's causing this temperature. I'll be back as soon as I can. If you're worried, press the buzzer.'

She gritted her teeth and went to find Andreas. She would have preferred to have avoided him completely but that wasn't an option. Bleeping one of the more junior members of his team would have taken time and she didn't have time.

And, anyway, she didn't really want one of the more junior members of his team.

She was worried about little Rachel. She needed someone experienced and he was the consultant after all.

She found him at the nurses' station, checking a set of X-rays, his shoulders impossibly wide as he stood with his back to her.

Libby swallowed and dragged her mind back to her work. She already knew he was a fantastic kisser. It was time to find out what he was like as a children's doctor.

'I need a doctor to see a new admission for me urgently.' Her tone was cool and ultra-dignified as she struggled to behave as though she hadn't kissed him senseless and then woken up half-naked in his spare bedroom. 'I don't like the look of her. Seeing that the rest of your team are elsewhere, I wondered whether you'd do it.'

Or was he the type of consultant who preferred to delegate to his staff? He turned and she backed away a few steps, watching him warily.

In work mode he suddenly seemed very imposing.

'I'll see her.' He flicked off the light-box and moved towards her. 'What's the history?'

Relaxing her guard slightly, Libby fell into step beside him as they walked back to the side ward. 'She was referred by her GP, but the letter just says that she's worried about the child's temperature. Not much else. The child is floppy, she's refusing fluids and I don't like the look of her.'

She'd been a children's nurse long enough to trust her instincts and her instincts were shrieking about Rachel.

'Great.' He shot her a wry smile. 'It's wonderful to be a GP, isn't it? If in doubt, refer to hospital and let someone else make the decision.'

'Before you insult GPs, you should probably know that my brother is doing a GP rotation—'

He lifted an eyebrow and his mouth twitched in humour. 'This is the same brother who forgot to buy you last night?'

Libby gave a wry smile at the reminder. 'I still have to speak to him about that. But despite his shortcomings as a brother, he's a very dedicated doctor. I expect he was caught up with a patient, which was why he didn't show up. Unluckily for me.'

'But luckily for me,' Andreas breathed softly, his eyes narrowing as he looked at her.

She blushed hotly. 'Stop it!'

'Stop what?' He dealt her a slow smile. 'Libby, I haven't even begun yet.'

Without giving her a chance to speak again, he walked into the side ward and introduced himself to Alison Miller before bending over the cot.

His swift shift from professional to personal and back again flustered her more than she cared to admit, and Libby struggled to concentrate as she followed him into the room.

Andreas didn't seem to be suffering from the same af-fliction. His eyes were on his tiny patient.

To the uninitiated it might have seemed as though he was just looking at the baby, but Libby knew that he was ac-cumulating vital pieces of information. She saw his eyes rest on the child's chest, assessing her breathing, saw the way that he noted her skin colour and the way she lay limp and unresponsive in the cot.

He lifted his head and looked at Libby, the humour gone from his eyes. 'Temperature?'

'Forty point seven,' Libby said immediately, and his mouth tightened.

'How did you take it?'

'With a tympanic membrane thermometer. I find it the best method in a child of this age.'

It gave an accurate reading of a child's core body tem-perature and didn't cause undue distress.

Andreas nodded his approval and looked at the chart Libby handed him, his eyes scanning the detail. Then he lifted his head and talked to the mother about the illness, questioning her about immunisations and family history.

As he finished scribbling on the notes, the baby started to cry fretfully.

Alison looked at them. 'Is it OK to pick her up?'

'Of course.' Andreas answered her with a reassuring smile before slipping his pen back into his pocket. 'Cuddle her. Then I will examine her. Libby, can I take a look at the letter from the GP?'

Libby handed it over. 'She did speak to Jonathon, your SHO.'

Alison scooped the baby out of the cot and looked at them anxiously. 'She said that it was probably just a virus but that it was best to be safe as her temperature was so high.'

It didn't sound as though the GP had even examined the child.

Libby glanced briefly at Andreas but his expression didn't flicker.

'Right.' He checked in the notes and frowned. As Libby had commented, there was virtually nothing in the referral letter. 'I'd like to examine her again, please. I'll go and fetch my things while you get her ready.'

Libby nodded and spoke quietly to Alison, explaining what was going on.

'Just hold her on your lap,' she suggested, fetching a chair to make it easier. 'Dr Christakos needs to examine her ears, and it's easier if you hold her like this, and like this…' Libby demonstrated and Alison did as she'd requested.

Andreas examined one of Rachel's eardrums and then waited while Libby helped turn the child round so that he could examine the other ear.

He was very, very skilled with the child. Gentle and swift, with no fumbling.

'Her ears are fine, and so is her throat,' he said finally, unwinding the stethoscope from around his neck. 'I'll just listen to her chest.'

Finally he rocked back on his heels. 'Her chest is clear so we need to start thinking about the less obvious.' He frowned thoughtfully and rubbed long fingers over his darkened jaw. 'Has she ever had a urinary tract infection?'

Alison's eyes widened and she shook her head. 'No. Well, not to my knowledge. Isn't that something that adults get?'

'And some children,' Andreas told her. 'It can be a cause of unexplained fever and I'm wondering if that could be the case with Rachel. There are some tests I want to do. I need to take some bloods and I want a urine sample.'

Libby pulled a face. 'That's never easy in a child of this age, as you well know, but I'll certainly try. She hasn't had a wet nappy for a few hours so we might be lucky.'

'Please.' Andreas gave her a nod. 'UTI is one of the commonest bacterial infections of childhood. It accounts for about five per cent of febrile illness. Rachel is very unwell and her temperature is very high. We need a specimen of urine urgently, and in the meantime we'll give her some ibuprofen to try and bring that temperature down.'

He scribbled on the drug chart and Libby went off to fetch the medicine and the equipment she'd need to take the urine sample.

Andreas caught up with her in the corridor. 'Your instincts are good. That child is very sick,' he said quietly. 'I'll give you an hour to get that sample and if you don't have any luck I'll have to do a supra-pubic aspiration.'

'An SPA?' Libby pulled a face. A supra-pubic aspiration meant inserting a needle into the bladder to draw off the sample of urine. It was sometimes used in very small babies when a sample was needed urgently and other methods had failed. 'Do we have to? That's invasive.'

'I'm aware of that.' Andreas ran a hand over his jaw, his expression serious. 'I'm also aware that the risk of renal scarring in infants and young children with undiagnosed and untreated UTI is high. I want to start antibiotics as soon as possible and I can't do that until I've taken a specimen. Call me if there's any change.'

Despite her best intentions, Libby found her eyes drawn to his mouth.

Being kissed by Andreas had been a totally new experience and for a moment she was lost, remembering.

'Libby?' His voice prompted her gently and she gave a start and her eyes flew to his, registering the gleam of amusement.

Damn.

He'd caught her staring.

She backed away, totally flustered. 'I'll get back to Rachel.'

His smile widened. 'Fine. Call me if you're worried.'

Trying to steady her thundering pulse rate, Libby turned and walked away from him, wondering how on earth she was supposed to get any work done with him smiling at her like that.

Determined to forget about him, she focused her attention on Rachel, trying to obtain the sample they needed so badly.

She didn't succeed and less than an hour later she was forced to find Andreas again.

She came straight to the point, her tone brisk. 'I'm worried about Rachel. Her temperature isn't coming down and I'm nursing her in a nappy and a sheet. I've tried to get a clean sample of urine but it's been a nightmare.'

Andreas frowned. 'Has she drunk anything?'

'Barely.'

'And she hasn't passed urine in the last hour?'

Libby shook her head. 'Her nappies are dry.'

Andreas nodded. 'I'll do a supra-pubic aspiration,' he said immediately. 'I know it's invasive but at least it's definitive and frankly I'm worried about her condition. We'll do an ultrasound to check she has urine in her bladder. I'll need a 21G needle—'

'I know what you need,' Libby slotted in, already on her way to gather the right equipment. She just hoped the new consultant knew what he was doing.

She laid up a trolley and was back by the cot minutes later.

'Someone needs to hold her very firmly in the supine position,' Andreas said calmly, using the ultrasound to check that the baby had a full bladder.

'I'll hold her,' Libby said immediately, 'and I know her mum will want to be with her. She's just nipped to the phone to call home.'

At that moment Alison returned and Andreas quietly explained why they needed to aspirate the bladder.

'Her temperature is going up and we need to obtain a sterile specimen of urine.'

Alison looked pale and tired. 'Libby was trying to get a clean catch.'

'I haven't managed it,' Libby said softly, 'and we really, really need to see if she's got bugs in her urine. In a child of this age this is the only reliable method and we need to send it to the lab before we start antibiotics.'

Alison nodded. 'So do it.' Her mouth tightened. 'Can I stay with her?'

'Do you want to?' Andreas spoke gently and Alison sucked in a breath.

'Yes. It's upsetting but I couldn't bear to think that I wasn't there for her when she needed me.'

Andreas exchanged glances with Libby and then turned away to wash his hands, scrubbing them methodically.

Libby prepared the trolley and then held the child while he cleaned the area with alcohol and allowed it to dry.

She watched as he inserted the needle gently, aspirating as he advanced it into the bladder, speaking softly to the baby as he worked. It was obvious from the skill and speed of his fingers that he'd performed the procedure many times before.

When he had the sample he withdrew the needle and his gaze flickered to Libby.

'Can you apply pressure to that site for about two minutes? Then cover it with a dressing.' He placed the sample on the trolley and turned to Alison. 'It's possible that she will have a bit of blood in her urine for the next couple of days so if you notice that in the nappy don't be alarmed. You can call Libby if you're worried.'

Libby lifted the gauze and checked that the bleeding had stopped and then applied a dressing. Then she swiftly dressed the sobbing baby and handed her to her mother for a cuddle.

'Just hold her for a bit and she should settle,' she advised. 'She's had paracetamol and ibuprofen so hopefully her temperature should come down soon.'

Alison looked at her. 'And the doctor really thinks that she has an infection in her bladder?'

'Yes, he does. The reason he wants to treat it quickly is because it can spread to the kidneys and cause damage.'

'But with treatment she should be OK?'

Libby nodded. 'Dr Christakos will probably want to do more tests to check, but you brought her in straight away so the chances are we've caught it before the infection has had time to spread.'

Satisfied that Alison understood the explanation, Libby followed Andreas to the nurses' station where he was tapping details into the computer.

'What happens now?'

'She's dehydrated so I'm going to put a line in and get some fluid into her. I'm also going to start her on IV antibiotics. When she's picked up a bit we can give her the rest of the course orally.'

'You're not going to wait for the results?'

He shook his head. 'It's important to treat her fast. If necessary we can change the antibiotics when the results come back. If the UTI is confirmed, we'll need to do more tests.' He didn't lift his eyes from the screen. 'All young children have to be investigated for vesicoureteric reflux.'

'So will you do an ultrasound?'

'Amongst other things.' He looked up and smiled briefly. 'Reflux and scarring can be missed by ultrasound in this age group so she will have to have cystography.'

'And you'll send her for a DMSA scan?'

'Yes. And, Libby...' He sat back in his chair. 'We need to try and get her to take oral fluids.'

'I know.' Libby nodded, well aware of that fact. 'Now we've got the urine sample I'll concentrate on that. I've explained the importance of fluids to the mother.'

'Is she breast-feeding?'

Libby shook her head. 'Bottle.'

Andreas finished what he was doing and stood up. 'Let's get that drip up.'

'I'll get a trolley ready.'

Libby spent the rest of the shift looking after Rachel, reassured by the fact that Andreas was within shouting distance if the baby's condition worsened. Apart from one trip down to the A and E department to assess a child, he spent most of the day on the ward, getting to know the children and meeting his team.

Libby tried hard to forget what had happened the night before but it was difficult to concentrate with those sexy dark eyes following her round the ward.

He was a man, she reminded herself firmly. Which meant only one thing as far as she was concerned.

Trouble.

Libby was updating Rachel's charts at the nurses' station when she glanced up and saw a young girl hovering by the entrance of the ward.

Her eyes widened.

'Adrienne?' She recognised Andreas's niece immediately, dropped her pen onto the desk and walked across to her. 'Hi, there. Aren't you supposed to be at school?'

The girl glared at her defiantly but her lip wobbled slightly. 'I've run away. And I'm not going back. *Ever.* I hate it there.'

Oops.

Her dark hair looked more unruly than ever and there were red rings around her eyes where she'd been crying. She looked very vulnerable and very young.

Libby leaned against the wall, her expression sympathetic. 'Do you want to tell me why?'

Adrienne shrugged and stared at her shoes. 'I don't fit in.'

Libby frowned. 'In what way?'

Adrienne didn't look up. 'I'm...different.'

'We don't all have to be the same. Being different can be good,' Libby said softly, but Adrienne shook her head.

'It isn't. It's horrible.' Her voice cracked slightly and she rubbed the toe of her shoe along the floor. 'I'm not trendy. I don't know how to be trendy. I tried to do my hair differently and wear make-up but Andreas made me wash it before I left the house. I hate him.'

Remembering the badly applied make-up, Libby privately thought that Andreas had made totally the right decision.

'How old are you, Adrienne?'

'Twelve. But I'm nearly thirteen,' she added quickly.

Libby nodded. 'It can be really tough being thirteen. I remember it well.'

'You?' Adrienne looked at her in disbelief and Libby nodded wryly.

'I had a terrible time. I was skinny as a rake, had a brace on my teeth and I wore glasses. And, to make it worse, my sister was stunning. Trust me—the other kids had a really big choice of names to call me. I know all about being different.'

Adrienne stared. 'But you're trendy.'

'Now maybe, but not then,' Libby assured her dryly. 'Who goes shopping with you?'

'*Yiayia*—I mean, my grandmother, and she's very, *very* conservative,' Adrienne said gloomily. 'Or Andreas, and he's even worse. He's so strict and traditional he won't let me buy anything remotely daring. Given the chance, he'd dress me in a sack.'

'Hmm, I can see that neither of those would be decent shopping partners,' Libby agreed, examining her nails thoughtfully. 'You know, if you wanted to, I could pick you up from school one day and take you shopping.'

The minute she'd uttered the words, part of her wanted to withdraw the offer. What on earth was she thinking? Offering to help Adrienne would inevitably bring her into contact with Andreas and she'd already decided to avoid him as far as possible.

Adrienne's gasp of delight made it obvious that there was no going back. 'You? Why would you want to do that?'

Because she was a total idiot and a sucker for any unhappy child.

Libby gave a weak smile. 'I adore shopping. Ask my brother or sister. I'm a shopaholic. There's nothing like a bit of retail therapy to cheer a girl up.'

Adrienne's eyes were huge. 'You'd take me shopping? *Really*?'

'Sure.' Touched by the girl's gratitude, Libby decided that she'd done the right thing. 'As long as you promise to smile and not argue with my taste. And then, when we've shopped, I'll do your hair. I'm great with hair. I've been practising for twenty-nine years on my own.'

Before Adrienne could reply, Andreas strode up and Libby stiffened, wondering how he'd react to the fact that his niece had run away from school. She remembered with appalling clarity her father's furious response when she'd done the same thing. *She'd never, ever done it again.*

But Andreas didn't look furious at all. He looked concerned.

'Adrienne?' His tone was incredibly gentle as he stopped in front of the trembling girl. He said something to her in Greek and she took a shuddering breath and looked him in the eye, replying in English.

'I'm so homesick. I want to live with you. *Please*, let me live with you—I won't be any trouble, I promise. I know that it's supposed to be temporary but I can't bear it. Please, don't send me back there.'

Swallowing back an unexpected lump in her throat, Libby glanced at Andreas, noting the tension in his wide, muscular shoulders.

'You're too young to be in the house on your own, *koratsaki mou*, and I haven't found a suitable housekeeper yet,' he said roughly.

Adrienne wrapped her arms around her waist. 'I don't care about being on my own. I'd rather be on my own than with those—those…' Her English failed her and she looked pleadingly at Libby. 'Tell him not to make me go back. *Please.*'

Libby glanced at Andreas helplessly. She really had no idea what to do or say. She knew nothing about the situation but she did know that Adrienne was obviously miserable.

Before she could speak, Bev hurried up, looking worried. 'Dr Christakos, A and E are looking for you. They've got a child with a nasty asthma attack. They want you down there urgently.'

Andreas sucked in a breath and cast a look at Adrienne. 'Of course.' He raked long fingers through his black hair, his frustration evident. 'Adrienne, we can't sort this out now. You'll have to wait in the staffroom until I finish.'

'Why don't I take her home with me?' Libby said quickly, putting a protective hand on the child's arm. 'I'm off duty now anyway and it would be much nicer for her. You can collect her from my flat when you're ready. Bev will give you my address.'

His mouth tightened. 'I'll have to take her straight back to school—'

Adrienne gave a moan of protest. 'No!'

'Adrienne, I have no choice!' He sounded tired and frustrated. 'If I could see another way, believe me, I'd take it. It's just for the short term.'

Libby wondered exactly what was going on.

Why was his niece living with him?

Bev touched his arm. 'Dr Christakos—'

'I'm on my way. Adrienne, we'll discuss this later.' His dark eyes rested on Libby. 'I don't particularly want her waiting around here so if you're sure it's all right, I'll take you up on your offer. Thank you.'

'You're welcome.'

She watched as he strode out of the ward and then turned to Bev who was watching open-mouthed. 'What are you staring at?'

'You.' Bev's eyes twinkled merrily. 'So you're definitely avoiding him, then.'

Libby gritted her teeth. 'This is nothing to do with Andreas.'

Bev nodded solemnly. 'Of course it isn't. I'm sure you'll manage to avoid him when he comes to pick her up *from your flat.*'

Libby glared at her friend. 'Mammoth rat factor, remember?' Turning her back on Bev, she held out a hand to Adrienne and gave her a warm smile. 'Come on. Time to go and raid my fridge I think.'

This had absolutely nothing to do with Andreas, she repeated firmly to herself.

Nothing.

CHAPTER THREE

LIBBY let herself into the flat.

'Let's get something to eat. I'm starving.' She dropped her keys on the hall table and walked through to the kitchen.

A dark-haired man with wicked blue eyes was lounging at the table, nursing a cup of coffee and reading a medical journal.

'You're in *big* trouble, buster,' Libby muttered, glaring at him as she tugged open the fridge door. 'This is Adrienne, by the way. Adrienne, this is my brother, Alex. Don't be taken in by the blue eyes and the charismatic smile, he's a total menace and I'm about to kill him.'

'Hello, Adrienne.' Alex smiled easily and then glanced back at his sister. 'Why are you going to kill me? You should be thanking me.'

'Thanking you?' Libby removed an armful of food from the fridge and slammed the door shut with such force that the contents rattled ominously. 'Where the hell were you last night?'

'Language, Elizabeth, language,' Alex reproved mildly, his eyes flickering to Adrienne. 'And to answer your question, I was in the middle of a tricky delivery. My legendary skills as a doctor were in demand. I was saving lives—snatching the innocent from the jaws of death—'

'Yes, yes, spare me the drama,' Libby interrupted him impatiently, and deposited the food on the kitchen table. 'For your patients' sake, I hope you're a better doctor than you are a brother.' She reached into the cupboard for some plates. 'Here we are, Adrienne. Help yourself. Food always helps in a crisis. Smoked salmon, ham, cheese, salad, chocolate, more chocolate…'

Adrienne sat down at the table and glanced between them, her face slightly pink. 'I'm not very hungry,' she said shyly. 'I'm really sorry if I'm in the way.'

Alex treated her to a smile that was guaranteed to weaken the knees of any female, regardless of age.

'You're not in the way. In fact, I'm very relieved you're here or my future on this planet would be in severe jeopardy.'

Libby noticed the way that Adrienne was staring at her brother and suppressed a groan.

Alex affected all women that way, no matter how young or old they were. He was lethal.

'So come on.' She looked at him pointedly. 'What happened? And don't give me any more of this "I was saving a life" rubbish.'

Alex leaned back in his chair and gave her a slow smile. 'I decided to do you a favour and let someone else buy you. Someone you could actually have a relationship with.'

Libby gaped at him. 'But that isn't what I want. You *know* I don't want a relationship.'

'Of course you do.' Alex suppressed a yawn. 'All women want relationships. It's in the genes. The minute you meet a new man you start scribbling his surname after your name just to see what it looks like.'

Libby was momentarily speechless. 'I don't do that! I don't want a relationship any more than you do!'

Alex regarded her steadily. 'Yes, you do, sweetheart. You're terrified of being hurt but deep down you believe in Mr Right as much as every other woman.'

'You're an insufferable chauvinist.' Libby was simmering and Alex looked amused.

'No, I'm honest. Men have different needs to women. We don't need all that "till death us do part" nonsense to enjoy a relationship. Even when we do end up marrying we only do it because that's what women expect. Not because it's what we want.'

Libby scowled at him, dying to let rip but constrained by Adrienne's presence. 'One day, Alexander Westerling, you are going to meet the woman of your dreams,' she muttered, her teeth gritted as she struggled with her temper, 'and I *truly* hope she refuses to marry you.'

Alex threw back his head and laughed. 'Sweetheart, the woman who refuses to marry me *is* the woman of my dreams.'

Libby glared at her brother with frustration.

He was devilishly good-looking and his ego had been fed a constant diet of adoring, hopeful women since he'd mastered the art of smiling. Consequently he didn't believe that there was a single woman he couldn't seduce into his bed if he put his mind to it.

But that was as far as it went. Libby knew that underneath the light-hearted banter her brother was icily determined never to settle down with one woman. She looked at him sadly, the anger melting away as she acknowledged that he was as much a victim of their upbringing as she was. When things had become heated between her parents, it had frequently been Alex who had intervened. The experience had left him with a serious allergy to long-term relationships.

She'd thought she was the same, but his words had kindled a doubt deep inside her.

Was she secretly hoping that Mr Right was out there?

Was she fooling herself by pretending that she wasn't interested in relationships?

Alex was looking at her steadily and she sensed that he knew what she was thinking. For all their petty arguing, they were extremely close.

'So tell me about the man who bought you,' he said, his voice surprisingly gentle. 'Rumour has it that he was smitten.'

Rumour?

Libby stared at him, wondering just how much he knew.

The hospital grapevine had obviously worked overtime. 'Did you know that Philip tried to buy me?'

'No.' Alex's smile faded and his blue eyes suddenly lost their warmth. 'I didn't know he was turning up or I would have been there. He and I need to have a chat.'

Libby watched as her brother's fingers tightened around his mug. For a brief moment both of them had forgotten Adrienne's presence. 'Defending my honour, Alex?'

'Maybe.'

Libby swallowed, touched by her brother's protectiveness. 'Would you have hit him?'

'Into the next county,' Alex drawled lightly, 'so maybe it's just as well I didn't go. I gather someone outbid him?'

Oh, yes. Someone had definitely outbidden him.

Libby stared at her plate, her mind suddenly full of Andreas. His broad shoulders, his powerful musculature and the aura of strength that surrounded him.

All her instincts warned her that he was the sort of man who broke hearts.

He was absolutely the last person that she ought to be daydreaming about.

So why couldn't she get him out of her mind?

'Lib?' Alex leaned forward, his blue gaze sharp. 'Come on. Tell your big brother.'

Libby felt her colour rise and cursed inwardly as she saw Alex smile knowingly. It was impossible to hide anything from him.

'He's not really my big brother,' Libby told Adrienne, keeping her voice light to disguise the hammering of her heart. 'We're triplets. He was born about three minutes before our sister Katy. I was last.'

Adrienne stared at them in fascination. 'Triplets? You lucky things. How wonderful to be one of three.'

'Not that wonderful,' Libby said, glaring at her brother, but Adrienne sighed wistfully.

'I think it's great. I would have done *anything* to have had a brother or sister and you've got both.'

Alex leaned forward, his voice gentle. 'You're an only child?'

Adrienne nodded. 'And my mum and dad died in a boating accident in Greece when I was tiny. I've lived with my Grandma for the past twelve years but she had to have a hip operation and now she's decided that she's too old to look after me now and that's why I've come to live with Andreas.'

Alex listened carefully to this tumbled speech and his gaze swivelled to Libby.

'And who's Andreas?'

'He's the man who bought me last night, Alex. Remember? I was for sale, and you were supposed to buy me.'

Completely unrepentant, Alex lifted a dark eyebrow. 'How much did he pay?'

'Andreas *bought* you?' Adrienne's eyes were like saucers and Libby suppressed a groan. She'd forgotten that the child didn't know the story.

'He just bought a date with me, that's all,' she said quickly, throwing a warning glance at Alex. 'The money was for a good cause. It was all very harmless.'

Except that the sum hadn't been harmless. He'd paid a small fortune for the privilege of spending an evening with her.

Adrienne's eyes were very round. 'Wow. That doesn't sound like him. Andreas is very picky about women. Especially women he doesn't know. He doesn't trust them. Grandma says it's because he's handsome, Greek and a millionaire,' she said ingenuously. 'They're after him for the wrong reasons. So why you were sleeping in our spare room?'

Aware of her brother's amused gaze, Libby gritted her teeth. 'It's a bit complicated.'

Alex drained his coffee-cup. 'I'll just bet it is,' he muttered under his breath, and Libby rolled her eyes in frustration.

Whoever thought it was great to be a triplet had never had a brother as infuriating as Alex.

'None of this would have happened,' she snarled, 'if you'd fulfilled your brotherly duty and bought me.'

Alex stood up, as cool and relaxed as ever. 'Of course, there's always the possibility that he might have outbid me if he's that rich.'

'You're filthy rich and I'm your sister!' Libby looked at him in exasperation. 'You should have been prepared to pay whatever it took.'

'To keep you out of the clutches of a handsome Greek millionaire?' Alex's eyes brimmed with laughter. 'I don't think so. I think he could be just what my baby sister needs.'

Libby stared at him, a suspicion forming in her mind. 'You did it on purpose, didn't you?' she said slowly, her eyes narrowing as she looked at him. 'You never intended to buy me.'

'I've always been very careful with my money,' Alex said lightly, 'and, anyway, there's nothing like a new love affair to take your mind off your old one. You needed a distraction from Philip.'

He lifted one broad shoulder in a careless shrug and with a conspiratorial wink at Adrienne he strolled out of the room, leaving Libby fuming.

He was *so* infuriating.

'He's *gorgeous*,' Adrienne whispered, her eyes still fixed on the door as if she was hoping that Alex would reappear. 'Really, really handsome. Those blue eyes are amazing.'

'He's dangerous,' Libby muttered, pushing her plate away and reaching for her coffee. 'Wherever he goes, he leaves a trail of broken hearts and sobbing women.'

At that moment her brother was *not* her favourite person.

'Like Andreas,' Adrienne observed wisely, and Libby smiled wryly.

She could imagine that it was true.

Andreas Christakos was staggeringly good-looking and if he was rich as well then that would be enough for most women.

But not her.

She was far too cynical to be taken in by a handsome face and buckets of sex appeal.

And she certainly wasn't interested in his money.

She stood up and smiled at Adrienne. 'Come on. Let's do your hair before he picks you up.'

Andreas rang the doorbell and glanced at his watch in frustration.

He was much, much later than he'd planned. Stabilising the little girl in A and E had taken a long time and in the end he'd admitted her to the ward, leaving instructions with the staff that they were to call him if there was any change in her condition. It had been a nasty attack.

The door opened and, instead of Libby, he found himself staring at a tall, dark-haired man with very blue eyes.

Andreas tensed and the warmth of his greeting froze on his lips.

This was not what he'd expected. It had never occurred to him that Libby could be living with someone.

His reaction to the evidence that she had another man in her life was so intense that he sucked in a breath as he felt a rush of that most basic of emotions—

Jealousy.

The man extended a hand, his expression friendly. 'I'm Alex—Libby's brother. You must be the guy who bought her. I tell you now, you should get yourself a refund. The girl's high maintenance and she costs a fortune in chocolate and shoes.'

Brother?

The tension left his shoulders and Andreas smiled

warmly. The knowledge that she lived with her brother and not her boyfriend caused him a significant amount of relief.

'Come on in.' Alex stood to one side to let him pass. 'The girls are in the bedroom. I don't know what's going on but there's lots of giggling.'

'It was kind of her to bring Adrienne home.' Andreas glanced around him, noticing the elegance of the spacious apartment. 'Your sister is good with children.'

Alex gave a short laugh. 'Better with children than she is with adults. Can I get you a drink?'

Andreas smiled and shook his head. 'No, thanks. I need to take Adrienne back to school.' He ran a hand over his darkened jaw. 'That's if I can persuade her to go back.'

At that moment a door opened and Adrienne came flying out, her face happy and smiling.

'Guess what? Libby's promised to pick me up from school and take me shopping one day soon.'

She had? Why would she do a thing like that?

Andreas hid his surprise. A day shopping with a twelve-year-old girl bent on choosing a totally unsuitable wardrobe wasn't his idea of relaxation. Why would Libby have volunteered for the task? She had no reason to want to help Adrienne.

He looked at Libby curiously but she carefully avoided his gaze.

Adrienne slipped an arm through his and looked sheepish. 'I'm sorry I ran away. Did you ring the school? Were they furious?'

'Yes, I rang and, no, they weren't furious. They were worried.' Andreas rubbed a hand over the back of his neck, wondering how he was going to help her to settle in. For all his experience with women, he knew nothing about twelve-year-old girls. 'It's a good school, Adrienne.'

Adrienne pulled a face. 'I suppose the teachers are OK but I haven't got any friends.'

'You've only been there for a week,' Libby said quietly. 'These things take time. Remember what we said.'

'Yeah.' Adrienne nodded and then looked at Andreas. 'Can we go for a pizza before you take me back?'

Relieved to have avoided a long drawn-out debate about whether she should go back at all, Andreas smiled. Whatever Libby had said to the child, it had obviously made an impact. 'Yes, we can go for pizza.'

'And can Libby come?'

Libby stiffened. 'I don't think—'

'Of course she can,' Andreas said smoothly, ignoring the furious look she shot him. 'It's the least I can do after the hospitality she offered you tonight.'

'Fantastic. I just need to say goodbye to Alex.' Adrienne hurried off towards the kitchen and Libby looked at Andreas angrily.

'I've already told you, I don't go on dates.'

'If you think that eating pizza with a twelve-year-old is my idea of a date, you're in for a pleasant surprise when I finally take you out,' Andreas drawled. 'You can relax. This is Adrienne's evening. You're quite safe.'

She sucked in a breath. 'Don't you understand no? Do I need to learn Greek?'

'It's just a pizza, Libby,' he said mildly, noticing with satisfaction that she seemed very tense. She definitely wasn't indifferent to him. 'Trust me, when we go on our date, we won't be eating pizza.'

'I won't go on a date with you.' Her eyes clashed with his and her blue eyes sparked. 'I don't want to go on a date with anyone.'

'But I'm not anyone.'

Her soft lips were parted and he could see a pulse beating in the side of her throat but she was still glaring at him.

'Sure of yourself, aren't you?'

He smiled, intrigued by the complexities of her character. On the outside she was prickly and sassy, but on the inside—his guts clenched as he remembered the way she'd handled the children—on the inside she was soft and all woman.

And he wanted her.

He lifted a hand and brushed her flushed cheek with a lingering touch that made her stiffen. 'Remember the fireworks, Libby.'

He could tell by the expression on her face that she didn't want to remember them. That remembering them disturbed her.

They took Adrienne for a pizza and then drove her back to school.

Libby helped to settle her into her room while Andreas went to talk to the headmistress.

Noting the awed expressions of her roommates as they stared at both Andreas and his incredibly sexy sports car, Libby privately doubted that Adrienne would have any more trouble fitting in, but she chatted away to the other girls, trying to help Adrienne bridge the gap.

When they finally left the school it was dark and Andreas drove back towards her flat.

'I owe you a big thank you.'

She glanced at him briefly, suddenly conscious of the intimacy created by the confines of the car. 'For what?'

'For being so kind to Adrienne.'

'She's a nice girl.'

His strong fingers tightened slightly on the wheel. 'I feel somewhat out of my depth,' he admitted wryly, sounding very Greek and very, very male. 'Dealing with twelve-year-old girls is new to me.'

His broad shoulders were only inches away from hers and she shifted slightly in her seat to try and create some distance.

'How did she come to be living with you?' Maybe if she stuck to neutral subjects she'd be able to forget how good-looking he was. 'She said something about her grandmother deciding that she was too old to look after her.'

Andreas gave a short laugh. 'My mother isn't too old for anything,' he said dryly. 'She was just playing games.'

'What sort of games?'

He hesitated and then cast her a smile. 'It's history now.' There was a brief silence and he returned his attention to the road ahead. 'I was very grateful for your help tonight. She seemed happy by the time we left her and that was because of you.'

Libby frowned slightly, wondering what he'd meant by the statement that his mother had been playing games. 'It's early days,' she said. 'It always takes a while to settle into a new school, particularly when you start halfway through a term.'

She gave a little shudder, remembering all too well the nightmares of school.

'You sound as though you're speaking from experience.'

'I am.' Libby stared out of the window into the darkness. 'We all went to boarding school. Alex was fine—he's as tough as nails—but Katy and I hated it.'

'Katy is your sister?'

Libby nodded. 'She works in A and E. She's married to Jago Rodriguez, the consultant.'

'Really?' Andreas pulled up outside her building and switched off the engine. 'I met him earlier tonight. Bright chap. But at least you and Katy had each other at school. Adrienne has no one. That worries me. And I hate her boarding. As soon as I find a suitable housekeeper she can live at home with me.'

'She's a lovely girl,' Libby said. 'She'll make friends, I know she will. She just needs a little more confidence and her appearance needs a bit of a tweak. I must admit I'm surprised that your mother expects you to keep an eye on her. You're a single guy and teenagers can be a handful at the best of times.'

'My mother is a master manipulator,' Andreas remarked. 'She is desperate for me to mend my wicked ways and settle down. She thought Adrienne might fulfil that purpose.'

Libby saw the amusement in his dark eyes and felt her heart lurch. It would be so easy to fall for him.

Why was she feeling like this? she wondered helplessly. She had more sense than to fall for a handsome face and a luscious body.

Maybe it was because he wasn't English. All that bronzed virility and exotic sexuality was getting to her.

But she had it under control, she told herself firmly, dragging her mind back to the conversation.

'So how does having Adrienne help?'

'She thinks it will curb my reputedly excessive lifestyle.'

'Oh.' Libby digested this. 'Evidently she thinks you've been dating the wrong sort of women.'

He threw back his head and laughed. 'She does indeed.' His smile faded. 'A bit like you. You've obviously been dating the wrong sort of men.'

Libby stared into those seductive brown eyes and swallowed hard. 'I've already told you, there's no such thing as the right sort of man.'

There was a slight pause. 'And you feel like this because of Philip or because of your parents?'

Libby stared at him. 'How do you know about my parents?'

'You told me.' He threw her an amused glance. 'You *had* drunk an orange juice so it's no wonder you don't remember.'

Libby gave a reluctant laugh and then slunk down in her seat. 'I don't want to talk about my parents.' She never talked about her parents to anyone. Why on earth had she mentioned them to him? 'I don't want to talk about any of it.'

'Not even Philip?'

'Especially not Philip.'

'Were you in love with him?'

He asked the question calmly and Libby looked at him, startled.

'No. I don't think so. But he was very persistent. Going out with him seemed logical.'

'Logical?' Andreas lifted an eyebrow. 'A true love affair should never be logical, surely. It is about emotion and losing control.'

Libby's smile faded under the intensity of his dark gaze. She'd never had a love affair with anyone.

'Well, it's probably my fault, then,' she muttered. 'I'm not great at losing control. In fact, I'm a control freak. I like to be in charge of everything that happens in my life.'

There was a long silence and then Andreas turned in his seat so that he was facing her.

'Powerful sexual chemistry is not controllable,' he said softly, lifting a hand and pushing a wisp of blonde hair away from her face. 'It's an intense emotional reaction that is beyond human explanation. Evidently you haven't felt that. Yet.'

The gentle brush of his fingers against her skin was unbelievably erotic and she felt excitement swoop inside her and concentrate low in her pelvis.

If sexual chemistry was butterflies in her stomach and difficulty breathing then she was feeling it now.

For him.

Dear God, she wasn't ready for this. After what had happened with Philip she doubted she'd ever be ready for it.

So why was she reacting so strongly?

Totally unnerved by the way he made her feel, Libby reached out and fumbled for her seat belt.

'I'm going. Goodnight.'

Before she could release the catch a strong hand covered hers and her head jerked up, her eyes clashing with his.

'Libby, it's OK. You can trust me—'

'No!' Breathing rapidly, she pulled away from him and

opened the car door before turning back to face him. 'Don't turn your lethal charm on me, Dr Christakos. Save it for all those millions of women that must be desperate for your attentions. I'm not interested. Thanks for the pizza.'

And with that she closed the car door behind her, hoping he couldn't see how much her knees were shaking.

CHAPTER FOUR

LIBBY arrived on the ward the next morning, determined to distance herself from Andreas.

She was finding it harder and harder to concentrate on her work with those sexy dark eyes seducing her every time she turned around.

There really was something to be said for having puny, ugly doctors around the place, she reflected. At least they made it easy to keep your mind on work.

If it was at all possible, she was going to bleep Jonathon, the SHO. At least he wasn't a threat to her pulse rate.

Even though it was early, the ward was already bustling with activity and Libby went straight to see little Rachel.

One of the night nurses was checking her temperature and glanced up as she saw Libby.

'Hi, there. I'm glad to see you. It means I can go home to bed.'

Libby smiled and looked at the child. 'How is she? She looks a little better.'

'Her temperature is down a bit so I think the antibiotics must be working. Dr Christakos checked on her in the night and he thought she seemed to be showing a response even though it's only been twenty-four hours. He thinks it's definitely a urinary tract infection.'

'He saw her in the night?' Given that he'd dropped her off fairly late, Libby was surprised to hear that he'd paid a visit to the hospital.

The other nurse smiled dreamily. 'He's *so* impressive. He was worried about the little girl who had the asthma attack last night. Apparently it was touch and go for a while in A and E and when he admitted her to the ward he was concerned that she could go off again.'

'So he came in to check her?'

'Yes. At about eleven o'clock.'

Just after he'd dropped her home.

Libby cleared her throat, trying to keep her voice casual. 'Has he been in this morning yet?'

Her colleague nodded. 'Oh, yes. He wanted to take some bloods from Rachel and while he was here he checked Marcus because he's due for discharge today.'

Libby hid her surprise. He certainly wasn't afraid of hard work. His team was really stretched and he was obviously more than happy to roll up his sleeves and help out.

On the other hand, his diligence was going to make it harder for her to avoid him. She could have done with a consultant who sat in his office and delegated.

'I'll finish off here. You go home. Where's her mum?'

'Having a wash. Apparently Rachel was awake quite a bit in the night so she didn't get much sleep.'

'Wet nappies?'

'Plenty, but I have to confess she didn't drink much in the night.'

Libby nodded. 'OK. I'll make a real effort to get her drinking today and then hopefully we can take that drip down.'

She smiled as Rachel's mother arrived back in the room, clutching a wash-bag and looking incredibly tired.

'Good morning. She looks a little better.'

Alison looked at her daughter anxiously. 'Do you think so? She certainly seems a little cooler but she was very fretful in the night.'

'It's early days yet,' Libby agreed, 'but hopefully she'll start to pick up today. We need to get her drinking so that we can get that drip out.'

The mother looked at her doubtfully. 'I suppose I could try her with a bottle now...'

'Let's give her another half-hour and see if she wakes up a bit,' Libby suggested, breaking off as Andreas walked into the room.

'Good morning.'

His voice was warm and intensely masculine and Libby felt her whole body hum with sexual awareness.

Colour warmed her cheeks. 'I need to check her temperature, but she's sleeping at the moment,' she explained quickly, as he picked up the chart. 'She seems to be picking up and I thought she'd be better off being left to rest. We'll try her with a bottle in half an hour.'

He scanned the chart briefly, looking at the readings the night shift had recorded. 'Let me know what her obs are when you've checked them and keep her fluids up. If there's a problem, call me. I've got to go down to A and E to see a child.'

Breathing a sigh of relief that he was going to be absent from the ward for at least a short time, Libby got back to work.

She checked on the patients who were her responsibility and then went back to Rachel and found her sitting on Alison's lap, looking much more alert.

'Oh, she's definitely a bit better,' Libby said, pleased by the change in the child in such a short time. 'I'll just check her temperature again and then we'll try and get that bottle down her.'

The temperature reading was down considerably and the baby took the bottle eagerly.

Alison was delighted. 'She wouldn't touch it yesterday so she must be feeling better.'

Libby nodded. 'We'll keep the drip up for now and I'll speak to Dr Christakos about it later. I expect he'll want her to carry on having her antibiotics into the vein for now, but hopefully if she carries on drinking plenty then we can take that drip out later today.'

Making a mental note to discuss it with Andreas next time

he appeared on the ward, Libby recorded the results and went to check on her next patient.

Her morning was horrendously busy and she was just starting to hope that she might actually be able to stop for a coffee when a five-year-old child was admitted with vomiting and fever.

Andreas appeared on the ward just as she arrived and Libby grabbed him immediately.

'Her GP sent her in because she's not keeping anything down and she's becoming dehydrated,' she told him as she briefed him about the patient. 'I've put her in a side ward for now, until we know what it is. If it's something infectious then we obviously don't want it spreading over the whole ward.'

He nodded and scanned the letter. 'OK—let's take a look at her.'

Melanie Palmer was lying on the bed, crying and clutching her stomach.

Her mother was sitting next to her, her face drawn with worry. She stood up when Andreas entered the room.

'She's been like this since yesterday morning, and she's getting worse,' she told them, her eyes pleading. 'What do you think it is?'

'I'm going to take a look at her now,' Andreas said immediately, walking over to the sink to wash his hands. 'How did it start, Mrs Palmer?'

The mother closed her eyes briefly, battling with tears. 'Sorry,' she muttered, 'but I've been up all night with her...'

Her face crumpled and Libby slipped an arm around her shoulders. 'Don't apologise. We understand how stressful it is when your child is sick. Take your time.'

'It started yesterday,' Mrs Palmer told them. 'She seemed a bit tired when I left her at Sunday school but nothing that made me anxious.'

'And when you picked her up, how did she seem?'

'She was white as a sheet and complaining of pain in her

stomach, but I assumed that was because of the vomiting,' Mrs Palmer said. 'I left it for a few hours, but then her temperature shot up and she seemed so poorly I called the GP. He just said it was a stomach bug and to give it twenty-four hours to settle.'

Andreas walked across to the bed. 'But evidently it didn't settle.'

'She was dreadful in the night. Moaning and crying and clutching her stomach. And her stomach seemed really swollen.' Mrs Palmer bit her lip. 'I didn't know what to do with her so I called the GP again this morning. I think he's probably going to strike me off his list for being such a nuisance.'

'You were right to call him again.' Andreas caught Libby's eye and she knew that he was thinking the same thing as her. That the GP had been too dismissive of Melanie's symptoms.

'Whereabouts was the pain in her stomach?' Andreas asked. 'Did she tell you?'

Mrs Palmer shrugged helplessly. 'Everywhere, I think.'

Andreas nodded and settled himself on the edge of the bed.

'Hello, Melanie.' He spoke softly to the little girl. 'Mummy tells me you've got a tummyache. Can I take a look?'

Libby watched him, full of admiration for the way that he dealt with children. She'd worked with so many doctors who didn't have the first clue how to relate to children. They just waded in with their tests and examinations and then wondered why the child wouldn't co-operate.

But fortunately Melanie was obviously smitten with the handsome Greek doctor.

She looked at Andreas trustingly. 'I've got a poorly tummy.'

Andreas nodded, his dark eyes warm. 'I know you have, sweetheart.'

'Are you going to make it better?'

'I'm certainly going to try, but you'll have to help me.' He lifted his stethoscope out of his pocket. 'First I'm going to listen and then you're going to listen.'

A brief smile touched the little girl's pale face and she lay still as Andreas started to examine her, whimpering occasionally with pain.

Libby watched as he used his fingers to gently palpate the child's abdomen.

'She has oblique muscle rigidity,' he murmured, 'which is a sign of peritoneal irritation.'

Libby looked at him, trying to read his mind. He obviously didn't think that Melanie had gastroenteritis.

Mrs Palmer was biting her nails in agitation. 'What does that mean?'

'I don't think she has a stomach bug, Mrs Palmer,' Andreas said gently. 'I think that she has appendicitis and unfortunately it has burst, which is why her stomach is so very painful and swollen. Libby, can you bleep the surgeons urgently, please, and then come back and help me? I need to get a line in. Mrs Palmer, when did she last have something to eat or drink?'

'She had a few sips of water in the night,' Mrs Palmer told them, 'but nothing to eat since breakfast yesterday morning.'

Leaving Andreas to finish his questioning, Libby hurried out onto the ward and rang the switchboard, asking them to bleep the on-call surgeons.

While she was there she gathered up the distraction box and the rest of the equipment she needed and then returned to the room.

Andreas was talking to Melanie, his deep voice gentle and soothing. 'I need to put a plastic tube in your arm, sweetheart.'

Melanie stared at him. 'Will it hurt?'

'Yes, a bit,' Andreas said honestly. 'But we need to do it to make you better.'

Libby looked at him. 'We could use a local anaesthetic cream.'

'No time.' Andreas reached for a swab and a venflon. 'It takes at least half an hour to work and I need to get this line in now. She needs to go to Theatre.'

Libby looked at the mother. 'If you find this too upsetting you could go and get a cup of coffee while we put the drip up.'

Mrs Palmer shook her head, her eyes glistening with tears. 'No. I can't leave her. Do whatever you have to do.'

'Right, then, Melanie.' Libby sat on the bed and put the distraction box next to the little girl. 'Let's have a look in here and see what we can find.'

'Balloons!' Melanie reached into the box and pulled out a pink balloon. 'Can I have it?'

'Of course. Why doesn't Mummy blow it up while we sort you out?'

Libby handed the balloon to Mrs Palmer who obligingly took it and blew.

Seeing that the child was distracted, Andreas searched for a vein.

'OK—squeeze there for me, Libby, and don't let go.'

Libby knew what he was saying. If they missed the vein on the first attempt, it would be doubly difficult to persuade a child of this age to co-operate, and it was distressing for everyone.

She hoped Andreas was good at finding tiny veins in tiny hands.

He was.

He swabbed the skin, grabbed the child's hand firmly and slid the needle in with the minimum of fuss.

Melanie was so busy watching the balloon grow bigger and bigger that by the time she opened her mouth to protest the cannula was safely taped in place.

Despite all her intentions about keeping her distance, Libby smiled at him. 'You're a genius, Dr Christakos.'

He grinned. 'So are you. I loved your distraction box.'

'It usually helps, but not always.'

Andreas turned to Jonathon, who had just appeared. 'OK, can you take some bloods while we're waiting for the surgeons, please?'

Melanie stared down at her hand. 'What does that do?'

'It means that I can give you medicines straight into your body,' Andreas explained, his voice gentle.

'I haven't listened to *your* chest yet,' she reminded him, and Andreas smiled.

'That's right. You haven't.' He undid a few of the buttons of his shirt and sat still while Melanie lifted the stethoscope to his chest.

Libby suddenly found she couldn't look away, her eyes riveted to the curling dark hairs that covered the hard muscle of his chest. He was incredibly masculine and she felt a kick of sexual reaction deep inside her. Suddenly she felt an overwhelming desire to touch him. To run her fingers over his tanned skin and downwards...

Shocked by her own thoughts, she dragged her eyes away, thoroughly relieved when the surgeons arrived.

Andreas smiled at the little girl and gently retrieved his stethoscope, totally relaxed as he briefly described his findings to Mr Jenner, the surgeon.

'I'll take her down straight away,' Dave Jenner said, after examining the child himself.

Libby collected a consent form and hovered by the bed, her gaze drawn again to the tantalising vision of Andreas with his shirt still undone.

He was powerfully built and strong and just that one glimpse was enough to make her imagine what the rest of him must look like.

She swallowed.

Still in conversation with Dave, Andreas lifted a hand and

casually started to button his shirt, pausing suddenly as he intercepted Libby's gaze.

His eyes locked with hers and something passed between them, a mutual acknowledgment of the sizzling attraction that seemed to envelop both of them whenever they were together.

Libby struggled to free herself from the intensity of his gaze and something of her disquiet must have shown on her face because his firm mouth curved into a smile so sexy that her knees shook alarmingly.

Bother the man!

He was totally aware of the effect he had on her.

Turning her attention back to the patient with a huge effort, she concentrated on getting the little girl ready for surgery.

'I don't want to take my pyjamas off.' Melanie wrapped her arms around herself and Libby managed a smile, pleased to have something to look at rather than Andreas.

'You don't have to take your pyjamas off, sweetheart. You can keep them on.' She examined the characters dancing over the fabric. 'I love them.'

'Daddy buyed them for me,' Melanie announced firmly, and her mother tensed.

'We're not together any more,' she muttered in an undertone. 'I suppose I ought to call him.'

'If you need to use a phone, I can arrange it,' Libby said quietly. They had plenty of parents on the ward who were separated or alone so she knew how hard it was when a child became ill.

'We'll see her in Theatre.' With a friendly nod to Mrs Palmer and Melanie, Dave Jenner left the room with his team behind him.

'You and I are going to play hairdressers,' Libby said cheerfully, reaching into her pocket for a band. 'I'm going to tie that lovely blonde hair of yours back. Is that OK?'

Melanie nodded and looked at Libby. 'You've got very long hair. Like a princess.'

Libby smiled as she checked that the child's name and hospital number were on her wrist strap. 'That's me. Princess Libby.' She gathered all the notes and charts together and finally plucked up the courage to look at Andreas. 'Shall we take her straight down?'

He nodded. 'I've done the consent form and everything else is ready.' He looked at Mrs Palmer. 'Try not to worry. Mr Jenner is an exceptionally good surgeon.' He sat down on the bed next to Melanie and took her hand.

'Right, Melanie, this is what we're going to do. There's something in your tummy that's making it bad, so we're going to take it away and then you'll feel better.'

Melanie stared at him, round eyed. 'Will it hurt?'

Andreas shook his head. 'No, because you're going to be asleep for a short time. And if it's sore when you wake up, we'll give you some medicine.' He glanced up as a porter arrived in the doorway, ready to take Melanie to Theatre. 'Ah—this nice man is going to wheel you downstairs now.'

He stood up and watched while Libby flicked the brake on the bed with her foot and manoeuvred it carefully out of the door of the side ward.

Melanie's face crumpled. 'I want Mummy!'

'Well, of course you do,' Libby said quickly, moving out of the way so that the child could see her mother. 'She's right here, sweetheart.'

Libby glanced at Mrs Palmer who was white-faced and tense. 'You can stay with her in the anaesthetic room until she falls asleep if you like.'

Mrs Palmer swallowed. 'Yes—yes, I'd like that.'

She stayed close to her daughter as they wheeled the bed into the lift and pressed the button for Theatre.

In the anaesthetic room a blond man was preparing things for the operation and Libby stiffened.

Philip.

Why did it have to be Philip who was the anaesthetist?

'This is Melanie Palmer,' she said coolly, her tone detached and professional. 'Melanie, this is Dr Graham. He's going to help you go to sleep.'

'Hi, there, Melanie.' Philip smiled at the little girl with the false cheeriness that people so often adopted with children. Libby couldn't help comparing him with Andreas who was a natural with children. He was honest and straightforward with them and had a warmth and strength that they seemed to find reassuring.

How could she ever have found Philip attractive?

Ignoring him as much as she could, she showed Mrs Palmer where to stand so that she could cuddle Melanie without getting in the way.

Philip wafted some gas under the child's nose and gradually her eyes closed.

'You can come back to the ward with me now,' Libby said gently, taking Mrs Palmer by the arm as Philip carried on anaesthetising the child. 'You need a cup of coffee and a sit-down. Mr Jenner will ring when he has some news for us.'

Philip glanced up. 'I'll pop up to the ward and see you soon, Libby.' His gaze was meaningful. 'We need to have a chat.'

Libby shot him a cold look but didn't respond. She didn't want to discuss her private life in front of patients or relatives. It wasn't professional.

And she had no intention of having a chat with him. If he appeared on the ward, she'd make sure that she was unavailable.

Once Melanie was safely under the anaesthetic, they returned to the ward and Libby settled Mrs Palmer comfortably with a cup of coffee before going to check on Rachel.

'Her colour is so much better,' she said, pleased by the way the baby seemed to be responding to the antibiotics.

'She's definitely improving. Has she been taking any fluids?'

Alison nodded. 'She took a whole bottle from me at eleven o'clock. She seemed really thirsty. It's the first time she's fed properly for days.'

'That's great news.' Libby smiled as she checked the baby's temperature. 'That's come right down, too. If she carries on like this we'll be able to take that drip out soon.'

'Will she need to carry on with the antibiotics?'

'Yes, but she can take them as medicine. She doesn't have to have them into a vein,' Libby explained, charting the temperature and noting the baby's respirations. 'Once we've taken that drip out she can have a trip to our playroom and we'll see if we can get her interested in some of our toys.'

It was after lunch when Melanie Palmer returned from Theatre.

'They took out her appendix and irrigated her peritoneal cavity,' Andreas told Libby as they settled the little girl back onto the ward. 'We'll continue the antibiotics and keep her nil by mouth until she's got bowel sounds.'

'Was it the GP's fault?' Libby asked softly. 'Should he have spotted it?'

Andreas pulled a face. 'In my opinion her clinical condition should have alerted him to the fact that it was something serious, but appendicitis in young children is notoriously hard to diagnose. Children tend to present late and a high percentage perforate before they get to see a doctor. In children under the age of three appendicitis is hardly ever diagnosed before perforation, but in her case...' He gave a shrug. 'Hard to say whether her GP could have diagnosed it earlier. I think he should have had a high index of suspicion but it's immaterial now.'

Libby was only too aware that Andreas had made his diagnosis within minutes of examining the child. But, then, she'd already seen enough of him to know that he was a very skilled paediatrician.

What with Rachel and Melanie, it had been a bad couple of days for GPs.

Mrs Palmer hurried into the room, her expression anxious. 'Is she all right?'

'She's fine. She's had painkillers down in Theatre so she's sleeping now,' Libby told her. 'We'll keep an eye on her and if she needs more, she can have them.'

Andreas explained the operation to Mrs Palmer and then moved towards the door. 'I'm just going to A and E to see a patient but you can bleep me if you need me.'

He walked out of the room and Mrs Palmer looked after him wistfully. 'He's a very good doctor.'

'He is, isn't he?' Libby agreed softly. 'He's a very good doctor indeed.'

Looks and a brain, she thought gloomily. A lethal combination.

She was in the storeroom towards the end of her shift when Andreas strolled up behind her.

'About this date you owe me...' His tone was smooth and enticing and she shivered with a response so powerful that she was forced to snatch in a gasp of air.

He was just *so* good-looking it wasn't fair. It would have been so easy to persuade herself that he'd be different.

Severely shaken by her own thoughts, she made a supreme effort to look bored. 'What date, Dr Christakos?'

Before he could reply, Philip's voice came from behind him. 'I was looking for Libby.'

Libby tensed in horror and backed away further into the storeroom but it was too late. He'd seen her.

Dealing Andreas a frosty glare, Philip walked into the room. 'This obviously isn't the place to say what needs to be said,' he muttered stiffly, 'so I just wanted to check you're still all right for the ball in three weeks' time.'

Libby's mouth fell open.

Did he seriously think that she'd still go to the ball with him after what had happened? The nerve of the man! Did he have no morals?

Wrestling with her temper, she struggled to find her voice. 'No, Dr Graham,' she croaked shakily, 'I'm *not* all right for the ball.'

Philip frowned and looked pointedly at Andreas. 'If you don't mind, I'd like to have a conversation with Libby on my own.'

Andreas didn't budge an inch, his usually warm dark eyes suddenly cold. 'I mind.'

Philip coloured slightly. 'We have personal matters to discuss—'

'We have nothing whatsoever to discuss,' Libby said tartly, relieved that Andreas hadn't abandoned her to her fate. 'And I most certainly won't be going to the ball with you.'

'Oh…' Philip looked slightly taken aback. 'But we agreed—'

'If you're short of a partner, I'm sure *your wife* would be happy to oblige,' Libby said sweetly, aware that Andreas had leaned his broad shoulders against the wall and was watching the encounter with an ominous expression on his handsome face.

Philip coloured unattractively. 'I've already explained to you that we're separated,' he muttered, and Libby lifted an eyebrow.

'Separated?' Sparks of anger lit her blue eyes and she curled her fists into her palms. 'Well, you certainly didn't look *separated* when I saw you the other morning.'

Philip gritted his teeth. 'I can explain, Libby. Listen to me—'

'No, *you* listen to *me*.' Libby took a step towards him, deriving considerable satisfaction from the fact that he backed away from her. 'You are a scumbag, Philip,' she said tightly. 'And if you want to talk to someone, I suggest you talk to your wife.'

Philip flinched. 'I can tell that you're angry and I can understand that you'd rather not go to the ball in the circumstances,' he said stiffly. 'It's going to take you a while to get over this.'

Libby's mouth fell open. 'Believe me, I'm over it,' she said acidly. 'And as for the ball, I never said I wasn't going. I'm definitely going. I'm just not going with *you*.'

Philip looked first taken aback and then horrified, obviously envisaging embarrassing scenes. 'You're never going to find anyone else to go with you at this late stage.'

Making an instantaneous decision, Libby flashed a dazzling smile at Andreas. 'I'm going with Andreas.'

She stepped closer to him and gazed into his eyes with all the adoration of someone who'd met the love of her life. 'You *did* manage to get the evening off, didn't you, darling?'

Andreas didn't hesitate. 'Of course,' he drawled, lowering his head and kissing her lingeringly on the lips.

Libby's brain ceased to function and she melted against him. She forgot Philip and she forgot the ball. She forgot that she was determined to resist Andreas. She was aware only of sensation. Delicious, tantalising, brain-swamping sensation.

And then Andreas lifted his head.

He brushed her cheek with his knuckles and gave a lopsided smile. 'Libby and I are hoping that there'll be fireworks,' he purred, laughter in his eyes as he looked down at her.

Stunned by the overwhelming chemistry between them, Libby flushed scarlet and Philip glowered at them both.

'Well, if that's the way you want to play it.' He turned on his heel and strode briskly out of the ward without looking back.

'You didn't have to kiss me,' Libby muttered, peering out of the room to make sure that Philip had left.

Andreas narrowed his eyes and surveyed her with all the lazy confidence of a man who knew he had the upper hand.

'I was trying to make it convincing,' he said helpfully, and she managed a scowl, even though her heart rate was still behaving strangely.

'Don't get any funny ideas, Dr Christakos. It's no big deal. I just needed someone to go with and you happened to be standing there.'

A lazy smile settled on his handsome face. 'Of course.'

'If I don't turn up, it will look as though I'm at home, pining for him, and I can't have him thinking that.'

'Of course you can't.'

She glared at him. 'This is *not* a date.'

'Of course it isn't.'

'It's just two colleagues on an evening out. Very platonic.' She bit her lip. 'No kissing or anything.'

His dark eyes gleamed with humour. 'No kissing?'

'Definitely no kissing,' she muttered, dragging her eyes away from his and concentrating on finding the dressing packs she needed. 'So, do you want to come?' She bit her lip, wondering why on earth she'd invited him. Talk about torturing herself. 'It's in three weeks' time. If you're busy it doesn't matter. I can ask someone else.'

Someone who didn't kiss like him.

Someone who didn't turn her brain to porridge.

He stepped closer and touched her flushed cheek with a lean finger. 'I'll take you to the ball, Cinderella, but I'm not promising to keep it platonic.'

Her stomach flipped over. 'Andreas—'

'Every time you see Philip, we seem to kiss,' he pointed out with impeccable logic, 'so we may as well both accept the way it's going to be. If we're spending a whole evening together and you're intending to convince Philip that you're over him, then I predict a significant amount of kissing.'

Libby closed her eyes.

What was she doing?

For a girl who was trying to avoid men, she was doing a pretty lousy job!

She suddenly decided that she needed an urgent talk with her sister.

CHAPTER FIVE

THEY were both on a late shift the following morning and met for a late breakfast in a café next to the river.

'Hi.' Libby dropped her bag onto the padded chair and stooped to kiss her sister. 'You look knackered.'

Katy gave a wry smile. 'Thanks for the compliment.'

Libby looked at her closely. 'Are you ill?'

'No.' Katy dropped her eyes and rummaged in her handbag for her sunglasses. 'Just tired.'

'Hmm.' Libby frowned and looked thoughtfully at her sister but before she could question her further, the waiter arrived to take their order. 'Two regular cappuccinos, please. And a chocolate brownie. I'm starving.'

Katy glanced shyly at the waiter. 'Actually, I don't want a cappuccino. Could I just have a mint tea, please?'

The waiter gave a friendly nod and Libby's eyes narrowed.

'*Mint tea?* All right, now I know there's definitely something going on. You always drink cappuccino. You're addicted to cappuccino.'

A soft flush touched Katy's perfect complexion. 'I'm just a bit off coffee at the moment.'

Libby sat back in her chair and stared at her sister. 'You're pregnant.'

Katy sank her teeth into her lower lip and adjusted her glasses. 'Libby, I don't—'

'I'm your sister,' Libby reminded her softly, leaning forward in her chair. 'Why can't you tell me?'

Katy sighed and removed her glasses, rubbing the bridge of her nose with her fingers. 'Because it's very early days

89

and I'm scared,' she admitted finally. 'I lost the other baby…'

'And you're afraid that you might lose this one too,' Libby finished, suddenly understanding why Katy had been reluctant to confide in her. 'Have you told Jago yet?'

'Last night.'

Libby grinned. 'I bet he was over the moon.'

Katy rolled her eyes and blushed slightly. 'You know Jago—macho Spaniard to the last. You'd think it was his achievement alone. A public declaration of his manhood and virility.'

Libby laughed. 'How many weeks gone are you?'

'Only six.' Katy let out a long breath. 'Ridiculous, isn't it? Getting excited so early. Something will probably go wrong.'

Detecting a hint of tears in her sister's eyes, Libby leaned forward and squeezed her hand. 'Nothing will go wrong, angel. It will be fine.'

'But the last one—'

'You fell, Katy,' Libby reminded her softly. 'You had a really bad fall. And it was more than eleven years ago. That's a long time.'

'Do you think so?' Katy looked at her, desperate for re-assurance, and Libby grinned.

'You're the doctor, honey. You should be telling yourself these things. Have you spoken to Alex? He's convinced he's God's gift to pregnant women at the moment.'

Katy shook her head. 'Not yet, but Jago and I are meeting him for supper on Friday. Any chance of you coming?'

Libby shook her head. 'I'm working. And, anyway, Alex isn't my favourite person at the moment. We've had a sort of falling-out. I don't think I could spend an evening in his company without physically abusing him.'

Katy sighed. 'I knew that it was a mistake for him to move into the flat when I moved out. The two of you are always arguing about something. What is it this time?'

'He didn't buy me at the auction,' Libby said darkly, and Katy's eyes widened.

'Was he supposed to?'

'Yes.' Libby scowled at the memory. 'I didn't want to be forced to go on a date.'

'And he forgot?'

'Of course he didn't forget.' Libby's mouth tightened. 'You know Alex. Why miss an excuse to wind me up? Don't worry. I'm going to the ball so we can all get together then and I'll tread on his toes.'

Katy stopped with her cup in mid-air. 'You're going to the ball? But I thought—'

'I know, I know.' Libby pulled a face. 'I sort of trapped myself into it.'

Katy put her cup back down on the table so hard that the tea slopped into the saucer. 'You're not going with *Philip*?'

'No!' Libby gave a shudder. 'I most certainly am not going with Philip. I wasn't going at all but then he implied that I was obviously too broken-hearted to go out so I was forced into a corner. If I stay at home he'll think I'm pining for him and there's no way I want him thinking that. Arrogant rat.'

'So are you going with the gorgeous Greek who bid a fortune for you at the auction?'

Libby stiffened. 'How do you know about that? Who's been talking?'

'The whole hospital,' Katy told her, her eyes amused. 'And can you blame them? He paid one thousand pounds for you, Lib! Everyone else was bidding tiny amounts.'

Libby shrugged carelessly. 'So the guy is rich. It doesn't mean anything.'

'In my experience, rich people don't throw it away,' Katy said mildly. 'It's the reason they're rich.'

'Well, I don't know why he spent a thousand pounds on me,' Libby said testily, picking up a spoon and teasing the froth on top of her coffee. 'Who am I to understand the workings of a man's mind?'

Katy gave a warm smile. 'He must have been pretty keen on you.'

'If he is, it's only because I keep saying no.'

'And why on earth do you keep saying no? Rumour has it that he's gorgeous.'

Libby thought of Andreas, remembering his luxuriant black hair and his incredibly sexy eyes.

'He is gorgeous.'

Katy looked baffled. 'So what's wrong?'

'He's a man,' Libby said flatly, putting her spoon down and staring at the patterns she'd made on the surface of her coffee. 'That's what's wrong.'

'So?' Katy finished her tea. 'You're twenty-nine, Lib. You can't carry on being this defensive. Eventually you've got to trust someone.'

'Why would I want to do a silly thing like that? It's asking for trouble.'

'I can tell you like him,' Katy said softly, and Libby gave a short laugh and picked up her coffee-cup.

'Oh, I like him. I like him a lot.' She felt things for Andreas that she'd never felt for a man before, and that worried her. It made her vulnerable. 'It doesn't change the fact he's a man.'

'Libby, not all men behave badly,' Katy said gently. 'You have to get out there and give it a go.'

'I've given it a go,' Libby said flatly. 'And I found him in bed with his wife.'

Katy frowned. 'But were you in love with Philip?'

Libby sipped her cappuccino. 'No,' she said finally, 'I wasn't. Which just makes me doubly determined not to get involved again. Imagine how much harder it would have been if I'd really cared. I'd be humiliated and broken-hearted, instead of just humiliated.'

Katy looked confused. 'So you're going to go through

life picking men you know you can't fall in love with? How is that ever going to work?'

'It isn't,' Libby agreed, 'but, then, I don't actually want it to work. I just can't deal with the pain that goes with relationships.'

'But maybe if you chose someone you really liked, the relationship might stand a chance of working,' Katy suggested logically. 'At the moment you're so afraid of being hurt that you pick people who you can't possibly fall in love with. You'll never meet Mr Right that way.'

'I don't believe in Mr Right,' Libby reminded her. 'He's a myth invented for children by the same person that thought up Father Christmas and the Easter Bunny. Personally I'd rather believe in the Easter Bunny. At least he comes armed with chocolate.'

But, despite her light-hearted words, she found herself thinking about what her sister had said. It was certainly true that she'd never really felt anything for Philip. Did she really pick men that she knew she couldn't fall in love with?

'You're so busy protecting yourself from hurt that you never go out with anyone remotely suitable. You're afraid of falling in love, Libby.'

Libby glared at her. 'I thought you were an A and E doctor, not a psychiatrist.'

'Today I'm your sister,' Katy said softly, 'and I love you. I want to see you settled with babies because I know that's what you want, too. I want to see you in love. And so does Alex, which was why he didn't buy you, I expect. He hoped you might meet someone, and you *have*.'

Libby stared at the river, watching the way the sunlight glittered on the surface. 'I don't want to be vulnerable and being in love just makes you vulnerable.'

Katy gave a humourless laugh. 'I know *that*. I know that better than anyone. I had such a dilemma when I met up with Jago again. He hurt me so badly the first time.'

'That was different. That was because our father meddled.'

'He still hurt me. Believe me, Lib, trusting him again was the hardest thing I've ever done in my life.'

'And Alex and I had to manipulate the two of you back together,' Libby reminded her dryly. 'You were going to marry Lord Frederick Hamilton.'

'I was marrying Freddie because I was scared of what I felt when I was with Jago,' Katy admitted. 'I was doing what you're doing. Running from being hurt. But there comes a point you have to take a risk with your heart, Libby. Otherwise you'll miss out on love. I shiver when I think what might have happened if Jago and I hadn't got back together. I love him so much. Without him, my life would have been so different. Empty.'

Libby sighed, acknowledging that she was envious of her sister's relationship.

'It's different for you,' she said gruffly. 'You and Jago are crazy about each other and you always were.'

She knew how powerfully Jago had affected Katy.

Having loved him, Katy had never been able to feel anything for another man.

But she herself never felt that strongly for a man...

Until Andreas.

Libby arrived on the ward for the late shift to find that Rachel had had her drip removed.

'She's doing so much better,' Bev told her. 'Andreas gave instructions for it to be removed this morning and she's having the antibiotics orally now.'

'Did the results of her urine tests come back?'

'Positive. It was a UTI.'

So Andreas had been right. Libby gave a reluctant smile. He might be good-looking and too pushy by half, but he was clearly a good doctor. Better than good. Hopefully, by treating the child so early he would have managed to prevent any damage to her kidneys.

'And how's Melanie this morning?'

Bev smiled. 'Doing very well. Her wound is a bit sore, obviously, but she's a lovely child. So cheerful.'

'Is her drip out?'

Bev nodded. 'She had bowel sounds so Andreas started her on sips of water last night and took her drip down this morning. I thought maybe you could get her to the playroom today.'

'Good idea.' Like all paediatric nurses, Libby knew how important it was that the children had plenty of opportunities for play. 'I'll get going, then.'

She started with Rachel, checking the baby's observations and noting with pleasure that her colour was good and that she was alert and interested in her surroundings.

'She's like a different baby,' she said to Alison, who nodded.

'I know. Those antibiotics worked like a miracle. Thank goodness the GP sent us in here.' She gave a rueful smile. 'He might not have diagnosed her correctly himself, but at least by admitting her we saw Dr Christakos. He's amazing.'

Right on cue, Andreas strolled into the room looking devastating in a blue shirt and well-cut trousers.

It was really unfair that any man should be so good-looking, Libby thought helplessly as she tried not to look at him. It was like having a job in a chocolate factory and being on a strict diet.

'She owes me a cuddle.' He smiled at Alison and scooped Rachel into his arms. He held her with the easy confidence of someone with plenty of experience with children, talking softly to her and allowing her to pat his cheek with her tiny hand.

'She likes you,' Alison said shyly, and Libby looked at him helplessly.

There seemed to be no age limit to the women he charmed.

Pulling herself together, she quickly changed the sheet on Rachel's cot and got her antibiotics ready.

'We'll give dose IV and then we'll take the venflon out and continue with the drugs orally,' Andreas said, still cuddling the child in his arms.

Libby tried not to look at him, busying herself with the various jobs that needed to be done and then excusing herself and hurrying back to the nurses' station.

Unfortunately he was right behind her.

'By the way...' he looked at her '...this trip you've got planned with Adrienne. She wants to know if you can do it in three weeks' time. She can't do it before that because there are things going on at the school that she wants to go to.'

Libby's face brightened. 'I'm delighted that she wants to stay at school.'

He gave a wry smile. 'Me, too. She seems to have finally made friends. Thanks to you, I think.'

Libby blushed. 'I doubt it. I was only there for five minutes.'

Andreas studied her. 'But some people make an impact in a very short space of time,' he said softly.

Libby's heart hammered against her chest. 'Three weeks, you say?'

'That's the Saturday of the ball so I suppose that may not be convenient. You'll want the time to get ready.'

'Believe it or not, it doesn't take me all day,' Libby said dryly. 'And, anyway, I need to do some shopping for myself, so that's fine. I'm really looking forward to it.'

'So is Adrienne.' Andreas surveyed her under lowered lids, his expression difficult to read. 'It's very kind of you to do it and I appreciate it.'

Did he think that was why she was doing it? To wriggle into his favour?

'I'm doing it for Adrienne, not you.' She looked him in the eye and then wished she hadn't. Head on he was dangerously irresistible.

Andreas smiled. 'Of course,' he said smoothly. 'Can anyone come or is it girls only? I could treat you both to lunch in the middle of what sounds like an exhausting day.'

Libby hesitated, knowing that Adrienne would like to have him there. It was clear that she was very fond of her uncle.

'You're very welcome as long as you promise not to give your opinion.'

He lifted an eyebrow. 'My opinion isn't valued?'

'Not by a twelve-year-old girl at boarding school,' Libby said dryly. 'I know what she needs.'

'And I don't?'

'You're a man,' Libby drawled, and Andreas gave her a smile so sexy that it melted her bones.

'I am indeed, Libby. And I'm glad you've noticed.'

Libby swallowed. Oh, she'd definitely noticed. It was hard not to.

The next three weeks passed so quickly that Libby barely had time to think. The ward was incredibly busy and Andreas was working so hard that she often went several days without seeing him, which was a relief because it made it easier to keep her mind on the job and not start dreaming about things she couldn't have.

They picked Adrienne up from school on the Saturday of the ball and drove into the centre of London.

'We're going to start by sorting out your hair,' Libby said, turning in her seat so that she could look at the child. 'I'm taking you to the best hairdresser in town.'

Adrienne's eyes widened and she lifted a hand to her unruly mop. 'I've never really had it cut before. I've just been growing it long.'

And it was badly out of condition and desperately needed

shaping, Libby reflected, although she kept those thoughts to herself.

'We won't cut it short,' Libby assured her. 'Trust me. It'll look great.'

She directed Andreas through some back streets and then showed him where to park.

'I'm amazed that there's somewhere to park this close to the centre,' Andreas observed, and Libby grinned.

'It's only for very valued customers. And I am a very, *very* valued customer.'

Andreas ran his eyes over her gleaming blonde curls and gave a wry smile. 'I'll bet you are.'

'A girl has to look after her crowning glory,' Libby said airily, pushing open the door of the exclusive salon.

She walked confidently across the marble floor and approached the reception desk.

'Morning, Francesca. Is Mario around?'

The girl glanced up and her face brightened as she recognised Libby. 'Well, hi, there!' A puzzled look crossed her face and she checked her computer screen. 'We weren't expecting you today, were we?'

'Not exactly.' Libby dealt her a winning smile. 'I'm after a favour.'

An extremely slim man wearing a pair of skin-tight, imitation crocodile-skin trousers minced across the salon towards her.

'Elizabeth Westerling, please tell me that this favour isn't happening on a Saturday.'

'Hi, Mario.' Libby followed and kissed him on both cheeks. 'You'll have fun, trust me.'

The man gave a dramatic groan and wiped a hand across his brow. 'It's Saturday, Libby. My busiest day. Everyone is clamouring for my attention—'

'But I'm not everyone,' Libby reminded him with a sunny smile that drew a wistful sigh from the salon owner.

'How can I refuse you?' He spread his hands in a gesture

of surrender and then froze as he noticed Andreas for the first time. His hands dropped to his sides and he took a step backwards, his eyes raking appreciatively over the other man's broad shoulders and powerful physique. 'Introduce me to your friend, Libby. *Immediately.*'

Libby laughed. 'Hands off.'

Mario's gaze lingered regretfully on Andreas whose expression was comical.

'Relax,' Libby said, still laughing. 'He's a brilliant hairdresser. The best.'

Mario was pacing the floor of his salon. 'Already I have your sister Katherine booked in and you *know* how fussy she is. Her hair has to look exactly so.'

'You've been doing Katy's hair for years,' Libby pointed out patiently. 'It won't take you any time at all. Now, listen.' She grabbed Adrienne's hand and pulled her forward. 'Mario, do you remember when I was thirteen?'

Mario shuddered at the recollection. 'You were all pouts and teenage rebellion and your hair never behaved itself. Not like your sister's.'

'Absolutely.' Libby smiled happily. 'Well, I've got another ripe case of teenage rebellion for you here. She's having trouble at school, Mario. I want you to transform her. She's going to be cool and a trendsetter by the time she leaves your salon.'

Andreas sucked in a breath and started to protest but Libby placed a hand on his chest.

'You promised not to interfere, remember? What do you say, Mario? Will you do it?'

Mario rolled his eyes dramatically and gave an exaggerated sigh but he stepped forward, loosening Adrienne's hair from the childish band she wore. He pulled a face as he pushed and pulled, feeling the hair and placing it in different positions, his eyes narrowed as he experimented with different effects.

'It is too heavy,' he murmured. 'It's concealing her face.

And she has a very beautiful face. It needs layers and texture.'

Libby beamed. 'My point exactly.'

Mario pushed, twisted and lifted for a few minutes and then sighed and looked at his receptionist. 'Rearrange my morning, Francesca. I'm going to be busy.'

He took Adrienne by the hand and led her through to the basins. 'We'll start with some serious conditioning.'

Libby followed and kissed him on the cheek. 'Thanks, Mario. You're a star. We'll go and grab a coffee and be back in an hour. And remember. She's not quite thirteen. I don't want lamb dressed as mutton.'

Mario looked affronted. 'You are trying to tell me how to do my job?' He clicked his fingers at one of the salon juniors who hurried across to shampoo Adrienne's hair.

'I'm not sure I should be leaving my innocent niece in the hands of that man,' Andreas muttered darkly, following her across the road to a café.

Libby laughed. 'Mario's great. But *you* had a narrow escape.' She shot him a wicked look. 'He really, *really* fancied you.'

Andreas shook his head disapprovingly and sat down at one of the tables on the pavement.

The sun shone down on them and the air smelt of fresh baking and garlic as the many restaurants prepared for their lunchtime trade.

Libby ordered cappuccinos. 'You look really tense. Come on, what's wrong? You're not seriously worrying about Mario, are you? Because you shouldn't. He really is the best hairdresser in London. People wait an average of four months to get an appointment with him.'

'Unless your name is Libby,' Andreas observed dryly. 'No, it isn't that. I'm worried that Adrienne will think that fitting in is all about the way you look,' he confessed, reaching into his pocket for sunglasses.

Libby sucked in a breath. Normally she found it impossible to look away from his sexy eyes, but now they were covered she suddenly found herself focusing on his dark jaw. He was staggeringly handsome and she could hardly help to notice the way that every woman who passed stared at him.

'Appearances matter,' she said, leaning back in her chair as their drinks arrived. She smiled at the waiter. 'Could I have a chocolate brownie, please?'

'Chocolate brownie?' Andreas lifted an eyebrow and she shrugged carelessly.

'A girl's got to have a vice. Mine's chocolate.'

Andreas gave a slow, sexy smile, his expression concealed by the sunglasses. 'And is that your only vice, Miss Westerling?'

'Yes,' Libby replied firmly, wishing that he would remove the sunglasses. It was unsettling not being able to see his eyes. 'But it's a serious one. Now, back to the subject of appearances. You're right that appearances shouldn't matter, but they do, I'm afraid. You know that as well as I do. People form an opinion about you within about thirty seconds of meeting you. And when you're a teenager, the way you look is part of being accepted. Teenagers have a uniform.'

Andreas lifted his cup. 'And you really think a new haircut will help her make friends?'

'I think it will be a start. The rest is up to Adrienne. Mmm. Yummy.' Libby licked her lips as her chocolate brownie arrived and Andreas tensed.

Feeling his gaze on her, Libby felt suddenly hot, every inch of her quivering, female body helplessly aware of the tension that simmered between them.

'D-don't look at me like that,' she muttered, and he lifted an eyebrow.

'Like what?'

His voice was husky and very male and she knew he was

teasing her. Suddenly she found she couldn't breathe properly.

Being this close to him affected her *so* badly.

He leaned forward in his chair, his voice soft. 'How do I look at you, Libby?'

His Greek accent seemed very pronounced and she dropped her eyes, concentrating hard on her cappuccino. It didn't really help. Even though she wasn't looking at him, she could *feel* him. 'You look at me as though you—you wish I was the chocolate brownie,' she said finally, and he laughed.

'My vice definitely isn't chocolate brownies,' he drawled. 'And we both know how I look at you. I want you, Libby. I've never pretended otherwise. And you want me.'

Her gaze flew to his. 'I don't.'

He shrugged carelessly. 'Yes, you do. You want me every bit as much as I want you. But you're afraid to admit it.'

Libby bit her lip. It was absolutely true. She *was* afraid.

She was afraid of what he could do to her. Of what he could make her feel.

'You are absolutely the last man in the world I'd have a relationship with,' she said flatly, glaring as yet another nubile female passed and cast a lustful glance at Andreas. 'Do you realise that every single woman who passes this table looks at you?'

Andreas removed his sunglasses and looked at her thoughtfully. 'But I'm not looking at them,' he pointed out quietly, his eyes dropping to her mouth. 'I'm looking at you, Libby.'

Her heart hammered against her ribs and she was consumed by a sexual excitement so powerful that she squirmed in her seat. She looked at him helplessly, thinking that perhaps it had been easier to control her feelings when he'd had the sunglasses on. He had the sexiest eyes she'd ever seen. What was it about him?

He was sitting on the other side of the table, for goodness' sake.

He hadn't even *touched* her and yet she could feel him with every inch of her body.

She swallowed hard and dragged her gaze away from his face. 'Well, I don't want you to look at me,' she said, stabbing her brownie with more force than was necessary. 'Do you want some?'

'What I want is for you to relax with me,' Andreas said, his tone amused. 'You are behaving as though I'm a lethal predator and there is absolutely no need. I want you and I refuse to pretend that I don't, but I have no intention of pouncing on you in the middle of the West End. I'll wait until you're ready.'

Awareness warmed her insides. 'You're awfully sure of yourself, Dr Christakos.' Her hands shook slightly and she placed the cup back down on the saucer. 'What if I'm never ready?'

He gave a slow smile. 'You will be. And in the meantime I'm enjoying the wait. It serves to intensify the satisfaction when we finally get together.'

His words hung between them and she stared at him wordlessly, wanting to say something cutting but totally mesmerised by the look in his dark eyes.

What woman in her right mind would say no to a man like Andreas?

He leaned across and helped himself to a piece of brownie. 'So, after this, are we shopping?'

He was so cool and relaxed, so totally sure of himself that she merely nodded.

'Yes.'

'For you or Adrienne?'

'Both.'

'Are you buying something for tonight?'

Suddenly unable to eat another mouthful, Libby pushed

the remains of the brownie to one side. 'Just shoes. I already have enough dresses.'

He lifted a dark eyebrow. 'And you don't have enough shoes?'

'A girl can never have enough shoes,' Libby advised him solemnly, standing up and dropping a note on the table to cover the bill. 'Come on. Mario should be just about finishing by now.'

And she needed a third person to stop her having indecent thoughts about Andreas.

CHAPTER SIX

As LIBBY got ready for the ball that evening, she reflected on what a successful day it had been.

Mario had worked wonders with Adrienne and she chuckled as she remembered the stunned look on Andreas's face when he'd first caught sight of his niece.

Mario had shaped and textured her thick dark hair so that it no longer swamped her delicate features. The new hairstyle cleverly emphasised the shape of her face and made her look exactly what she was. A child on the verge of womanhood.

Thrilled by her own reflection, Adrienne had spent the rest of the trip gazing at her reflection in shop windows.

Libby had dragged her into several of her favourite shops and bought a selection of strap tops and trendy cotton separates that complemented Adrienne's slim figure without making her seem older than she was.

By the time they'd returned her to school, she'd been bubbling with excitement and confidence.

And now it was her turn, Libby thought, reaching into her wardrobe for the dress she wanted.

It was made of pale gold silk and it fell from tiny straps right down to the floor.

And she loved it.

With a smile of satisfaction she slipped into the dress and slid her feet into the gold shoes that she'd found in a tiny shop in one of London's most exclusive shopping areas. They matched the dress perfectly.

She pinned her blonde curls on top of her head, leaving a few tendrils hanging loose around her face, and carefully applied her lipstick.

Satisfied with the result, she reached for her wrap and glanced at her watch as the doorbell went.

Alex had left to collect his date half an hour earlier so she knew it had to be Andreas.

She walked to the door on shaking legs and paused for a moment. Her heart rate accelerated dramatically and excitement curled in the pit of her stomach.

She closed her eyes briefly, wondering why on earth she'd invited the man. She was playing with fire.

Andreas Christakos could hurt her badly.

Taking a steadying breath, she opened the door, trying to control her reaction as she saw him.

Damn.

She should have known that the man would have looked spectacular in formal dress.

She bit back a groan. The truth was Andreas would look spectacular whatever he wore.

He lounged in her doorway, confident, sexy and so masculine that it took her breath away.

He was all temptation and trouble and she'd elected to spend the evening with him.

Great.

'Hi, there.' She sounded breathless and hated herself for it. She hoped he wasn't any good at reading body language but her instincts said that he would be. This man knew everything there was to know about women.

His eyes slid slowly over her and finally he spoke. 'You look sensational.'

Suddenly she wished she'd chosen to wear a different dress. Something that covered her up. Something that would protect her from the way he was looking at her. The dress she'd chosen skimmed her womanly curves and seemed demure enough from the front, but the back was a different matter, and she found herself wishing that she didn't have to turn around.

He was looking at her quizzically. 'Are you ready?'

'I need to fetch my bag.' Which meant turning round.

His gaze didn't shift from hers. 'Fine.'

Swallowing hard, she backed away from him and his eyes narrowed.

'Is something wrong?'

'No.' This was utterly ridiculous! She took a deep breath and turned around, walking quickly to her room to collect her bag.

She returned in seconds. 'I'm ready.'

He didn't answer and slowly she lifted her gaze to his.

'Well, now I know why you were reluctant to turn around,' he said hoarsely, his dark eyes holding hers. 'That dress should carry a health warning. Shall we go?'

He placed a hand on her bare back and it was as if she'd drunk champagne on an empty stomach. Her legs trembled and her head swam. She was acutely conscious of every inch of him as they made their way down in the lift and climbed into the car he had waiting.

It was a warm summer evening but suddenly Libby found herself shivering.

His gaze settled on her face. 'Are you cold?'

Libby shook her head, knowing that she'd never be able to convince him that she was cold.

She wasn't cold. She was just suffering from an acute attack of out-of-control hormones. No man had ever affected her this way before. She'd never experienced this stomach-curling excitement that she felt with him.

'So why are you shivering, *agape mou*?'

She turned to look at him and gave a moan as his mouth descended on hers.

His kiss was slow and erotic and within seconds she was clinging to him, wriggling closer, her whole body throbbing with a heat and desire that was totally unfamiliar.

When he finally lifted his head, her heart was thundering in her chest.

'I've ruined your lipstick,' he said huskily, his eyes resting on her swollen mouth. 'I'm sorry.'

She swallowed hard and reached for her bag. 'J-just don't do it again,' she stammered, ignoring his low chuckle.

Who was she kidding?

Kissing Andreas was like taking a trip to heaven.

Given the choice, she'd happily spend the rest of her life doing nothing else.

They arrived at the hotel and joined the rest of the guests on the terrace where they were drinking champagne.

Libby immediately caught sight of Katy and Alex with their partners. Anxious to be in a group as a method of self-protection, she took Andreas by the arm and walked across to them.

Katy was looking elegant and classy in a long black dress, her blonde hair swept up on top of her head. She had more colour in her cheeks than the last time they'd met and Libby leaned forward to kiss her and then turned to Jago, Katy's husband.

'Congratulations,' she whispered, as she stood on tiptoe to kiss him.

Then she shook hands with Alex's date for the night, a cool-eyed blonde who was a clone of all the women that Alex dated.

Libby smiled politely, noted that the girl's name was Eva and wondered whether she knew that Alex would be seeing someone else within three months. He never dated anyone for longer than that. He was more wary of commitment than she was.

She introduced Andreas and instantly he and Jago started talking about a case they'd had in A and E the previous day.

'No talking shop,' Katy reproved mildly. 'This is supposed to be the one night of the year when we have an evening out without discussing medicine. Anyway, it's time to sit down. We're all on the same table.'

They moved into the ballroom, found their table and Libby seated herself between Alex and Andreas.

She was painfully conscious of how close he was, his lean, brown hand resting on the table only inches from hers, his muscular thigh resting alongside hers and the width of his shoulders under the jacket he wore.

Although they talked and laughed with everyone on the table, she was always aware of him next to her.

From time to time during the meal she caught him watching her and knew that he was playing a waiting game. Andreas was well aware of the effect he had on her and he was biding his time, knowing that the feelings inside her were heating to dangerous levels. It was psychological seduction, mind games designed to drive her slowly but surely to a point of desperation.

Her insides were so churned up by the way he made her feel that Libby lost her appetite. She pushed her food unenthusiastically around her plate and Alex looked at her with a raised eyebrow.

'Following the Hollywood diet, Lib?'

She gave a wan smile. 'I'm just not that hungry.'

'Or, at least, not for food,' Alex murmured softly, his eyes flickering past her to Andreas who was engaged in conversation with Katy, seated to his right. 'I've never seen you like this before. It must be love.'

Love?

Libby's eyes widened and she looked at him in horror. Of course it wasn't love! She'd never be so foolish as to fall in love with a man like Andreas. He was every woman's fantasy and she had no doubt that she was just a temporary interest.

'It's not love,' she said in a strangled voice. 'I've never been in love.'

Alex shrugged. 'Well, something's wrong. That's chocolate mousse sitting in front of you and you're not showing any interest in it.'

Libby looked at her plate and realised that she hadn't even seen the chocolate mousse arrive. Normally she would have devoured it, but tonight she just couldn't face food of any sort.

Not even chocolate.

'If you're off chocolate, it must be serious,' Alex said dryly, glancing from her to the untouched mousse. 'It's either love or gastroenteritis. Trust me, I'm a doctor. I know about these things.'

Thoroughly unsettled, Libby glared at him. 'You're a troublemaker and can we, please, change the subject?' Her eyes flickered past him to Eva who was talking to a colleague of Alex's from A and E. 'Anyway, you're a fine one to talk. She hasn't stopped drooling over you all night.'

'She'll get over it,' Alex drawled lightly, reaching for his wine.

Libby shook her head slightly, wondering what sort of female it would take to shake her brother out of his customary cool.

'Don't you feel guilty about going through life breaking hearts?' Libby muttered in an undertone. 'It's men like you that have made me the woman I am today.'

Alex lifted a dark eyebrow. 'A crazy, shoe-mad chocoholic?'

'You can joke,' Libby said loftily, 'but you know it's true.'

Alex frowned. 'It's not true. I've never deceived a woman in my life.' His tone was maddeningly cool. 'I'm always totally honest with them. And I'm completely faithful when I'm with a woman.'

'Which is for a maximum of three months,' Libby reminded him tartly.

Alex shrugged his broad shoulders dismissively. 'So? I've never met a woman I wanted to wake up next to every day for the rest of my life.'

Libby rolled her eyes. 'Well, I'm just glad I'm your sister.'

Alex smiled the smile that stopped women in their tracks. 'What you're saying is that I'm so irresistible that if you weren't my sister you'd be in love with me.' His blue eyes gleamed with amusement. 'Go on, admit it.'

Libby's mouth fell open and she was about to deliver a suitable retort when Katy intervened.

'I can't hear what the pair of you are talking about, but I know you're quarrelling, so stop it,' she admonished gently from across the table. 'Alex, stop teasing Libby!'

'Me?' Alex lifted a hand to his broad chest, his expression hurt. 'I would *never* tease my sister. I have the utmost respect for my sister.'

'Alex…' Libby's tone was sugar sweet and she lifted a hand to her plate, her eyes sparkling with mischief as she looked thoughtfully at her brother's pristine white dress shirt. 'I've just thought of a use for this chocolate mousse.'

'Will you two stop it?' Katy stared at them, aghast, and then shot an embarrassed look towards Andreas. 'I'm so sorry. What must you be thinking? They love each other really, it's just that they can't seem to help winding each other up. They're always the same.'

Andreas laughed, totally relaxed. 'Don't apologise. Their conversation is very entertaining.' His eyes rested on Libby thoughtfully. 'And illuminating.'

Libby forgot about the chocolate mousse and Alex's shirt and looked at him in horror. Just how much of the conversation had he overheard? Had he heard Alex suggesting that she was in love? She sincerely hoped not.

The chat started up again but Libby found herself staring at Andreas, trapped by the look in his stunning dark eyes. His gaze was intense and focused and there was no way he was letting her look away.

'So why haven't you eaten anything tonight, Libby?' His

firm mouth shifted slightly at the corners. 'Is it the Hollywood diet—or is it something else?'

Libby gritted her teeth and resisted the temptation to slide under the table to hide her embarrassment. He'd obviously heard everything.

She closed her eyes and cursed her brother and his big mouth.

It was becoming harder and harder to keep Andreas at a distance. How was she going to manage it if he thought that she was so affected by him that she was off her food?

'I'm just not that hungry,' she mumbled, pushing her plate away from her and accepting the coffee that the waiter offered. 'I never eat much at these things. Hard to make a serious impact on the dance floor if you're full of food.'

Andreas glanced towards the band, which was playing something with a pounding rhythm. 'If you're aiming to make a serious impact, we'd better get started.' He stood up, broad-shouldered and confident, and extended a hand. 'Dance, Libby?'

Aware that the rest of the people at the table were watching her expectantly, Libby let him pull her to her feet.

It shouldn't be a problem, she reassured herself. The band was playing fast stuff. Nothing that required the slightest bit of physical contact.

But the minute they reached the dance floor she realised that she'd made a major misjudgement.

Andreas was a fantastically good dancer. He closed strong fingers around hers and swung her against him, picking up the rhythm of the music and controlling her moves like a master.

Totally seduced by the pounding beat of the music and his strong lead, Libby let herself go, swaying and spinning, moving away from him and then back again, feeling his hard, muscular strength against her heated body.

A natural dancer, Libby ignored the fact that her hair had

escaped from the pin on top of her head and was flying around her face as he spun her around the dance floor.

She was having far too much fun to care.

It was only when the music ended and applause broke out around them that she realised that they were the only ones that were dancing.

Suddenly self-conscious, she made to retreat to their table but Andreas laughed and hauled her against him.

'Don't you dare. We haven't even begun yet.'

This time several couples joined them on the dance floor, obviously inspired by their exhibition.

They danced continuously until finally the band shifted tempo and played something slow and seductive. On the dance floor the lighting softened and suddenly the atmosphere became more intimate.

'You didn't tell me you could dance,' Libby said breathlessly, pink and laughing from the exertion. 'That was fantastic.'

'I'm Greek,' he reminded her silkily. 'All Greeks can dance.'

Without giving her a chance to argue, he curved a strong arm around her, pulling her firmly against him, and Libby put a hand on his shoulder, feeling the hardness of muscle thinly disguised by the fabric of his shirt. Disconcerted by the way he made her feel, she tried to keep up the conversation.

'I thought you did traditional dancing with lots of plate-smashing.'

'That, too. Now stop talking, Libby.'

He pulled her closer, sliding an arm around her hips so that she was pressed against him.

Aware of every incredible inch of him, Libby dipped her head against his chest and closed her eyes, breathing in his male scent and the subtle hint of aftershave.

The intensity of her body's response shocked her. Butterflies erupted in her stomach and she was sure that he must be able to feel her body quivering. Every part of her felt sensitive. She was incredibly aware of every inch of his body. Unable to help herself, she pressed closer still and he immediately lifted a hand to her face, sliding his lean fingers around her jaw and forcing her to look at him.

The laughter had long since faded and the emotion sizzling between them was intense sexual excitement. An overwhelming acknowledgement of the astonishing chemistry between them. Skin brushed against skin, breath mingled unsteadily and the heat became almost intolerable.

'P-people are staring at us,' Libby stammered, shivering as she felt his thumb trace the fullness of her lower lip.

'Let them stare,' Andreas murmured softly, supremely indifferent to the curious glances they were receiving. 'On the other hand, I could do with some fresh air. How about you?'

Libby nodded. What she really needed was a cold shower, but fresh air would probably do.

His long fingers closed around her wrist and he strode off the dance floor towards one of the exits, dragging her after him.

Feeling that just about everyone was probably staring at them, Libby didn't look left or right.

'You're behaving like a caveman,' she muttered, mortified by what people must be thinking. 'This isn't very politically correct.'

He shot her a sizzling smile of pure sexual invitation. 'That's because I'm Greek,' he drawled in that dark tone that sent shivers down her spine. 'We're not very good at being politically correct.'

He led her out into the grounds, past the small lights that added a subtle glow to the darkness and illuminated the surroundings just enough to allow them to find their way. After the heat and noise of the ballroom the air was incredibly cool and peaceful.

A few couples were seated at tables outside, but Andreas

ignored them and didn't break his stride, taking her across
the grass and down towards the ornamental lake.

Finally he slowed down and took a deep breath. 'That's
better. It was very hot in there, *agape mou.*'

Libby looked at him shyly. 'What does that mean?'

He didn't answer her and, seeing the lights of the ballroom and hearing the music fading into the background,
Libby felt suddenly vulnerable. All of a sudden it was just
a woman alone with a man in the incredible intimacy created by the semi-darkness.

She felt breathlessly unsure as he led her down some steps
and through some trees and suddenly they were on the edge
of the lake.

'Oh!' She stopped dead, enchanted by the moonlight
flickering on the nearly still water. 'It's magical. How did
you know it was here?'

Andreas maintained his grip on her wrist. 'I saw it from
the terrace when we were drinking champagne earlier.'

After the heat and noise of the ballroom it felt wonderfully peaceful and she stood for a moment, enjoying the
silence, breathlessly aware of his powerful presence next to
her. Even without turning her head, she sensed that he was
looking at her and she felt her heart thud against her chest
in a frenzy of anticipation. His fingers hadn't moved from
her wrist but she could feel his touch with every part of her
body.

'Libby?'

All he did was say her name but his soft tone brushed
over her nerve endings and made her shiver with a sexual
excitement that was as intense as it was unfamiliar.

Barely breathing, she turned to face him and collided with
the raw passion in his dark eyes. Suddenly there were butterflies in her stomach and her head felt woolly. Somewhere
in the back of her mind she registered that she was supposed
to be resisting him but for the life of her she couldn't quite
remember why.

Why would any woman in her right mind want to resist Andreas?

He was still looking down at her, dark eyes slightly narrowed in a scrutiny so shockingly sexual that she felt dizzy.

By the time he finally lowered his head to hers she was quivering with expectation, longing for his touch, and the moment his mouth found hers she moaned and lifted her hands to his chest, curling her fingers into the front of his shirt, feeling the warmth of his chest through the thin fabric.

He kissed her slowly, teasing her mouth with gentle expertise until she pressed against him, desperate for him to deepen the kiss. Every seductive stroke of his tongue drove her demented with longing and she wrapped her arms round his neck and pulled him closer.

Still kissing her, Andreas shrugged off his jacket, letting it fall onto the grass, and then his arms came round her, hauling her close.

She felt his warm hands slide down her bare back, pressing her against him, making her aware of the intensity of his desire.

And suddenly she wanted more.

He wasn't moving fast enough.

Her arms dropped from his neck to his waist and she wrenched at his shirt, tearing buttons in her need to get closer to him.

She felt his hands slide the straps of her dress down her arms, baring her breasts to the cool night air. He dragged his mouth from hers and trailed kisses down her bare neck and she threw her head back, her eyes closed, all thought suspended as she felt him move lower. Then the coolness was replaced by warmth as he took her in his mouth, teasing her nipple until she cried out, overwhelmed by the exquisite agony of his touch.

His hands were on her thighs, drawing the silken fabric of her dress upwards, and she moved her hips against him, encouraging the contact that he was clearly seeking.

And then his mouth was on hers again and he lowered her to the ground. The damp grass cooled her heated skin and she lay breathless on the bed that nature had provided, aware of nothing except the aching need low in her pelvis and the weight of his body on hers.

His breathing was ragged and he delved deep into her mouth with his tongue, shifting his body so that he lay between her thighs.

Totally abandoned, Libby moaned and kissed him back, arching against him, burning with excitement when he finally touched her where she was aching to be touched.

She gasped his name, wanting more, needing more, totally consumed by the excitement that he'd unleashed.

He lifted his head briefly and she felt his hesitation.

'Andreas…' Her hoarse plea seemed to be the only encouragement he needed because he stared down into her eyes as he adjusted his position and dealt with the thin silk of her panties.

She was dimly aware of his strong fingers biting into her thigh, of the scrape of his rough jaw against her face and then he was there, entering her with a smooth thrust, trapping her gasp of ecstasy with his mouth. She felt his urgency as he drove deep inside her, filling her, increasing her level of arousal with each expert thrust. Dizzy with excitement, her fingers dug into the hard muscles of his back, and she arched up against him, unconsciously drawing him closer still.

The darkness ceased to exist, as did the lake and the press of the cool grass against her back. There was nothing except Andreas and the way he made her feel.

And Libby knew that nothing in her life had ever felt so totally right.

'Open your eyes.' His rough command penetrated the fog of sensation that held her in its grip and she did as he ordered, drowning in the raw sexual hunger that she read in his gaze.

Clashing with the heat of his eyes merely heightened the excitement and she struggled to breathe as he drove them both to such terrifying heights that the only way to go was down. She fell headlong into an explosive climax, aware that she was taking him with her, submitting to the wild, unfamiliar sensations that scorched her body.

Totally wiped out by the intensity of the experience, Libby closed her eyes and lay still, aware of the weight of his body on hers, his solid strength pinning her to the grass.

She could have stayed there for ever, feeling the rhythmic thud of his heart against hers, the warmth of his breath against her neck as both of them slowly returned to the present.

She was aware of the uneven ground pressing into her back through the soft grass, of the cool night air brushing her bare, heated skin, but most of all she was aware of Andreas.

He was still wearing his shirt but it hung open where she'd all but torn it apart in her haste to undress him and the edges trailed around her, hiding her semi-nakedness. Somewhere nearby lay his jacket, carelessly discarded in their fevered desperation to remove all barriers.

He muttered something in Greek that she didn't understand and shifted his weight, rolling onto his side and taking her with him.

He stroked her tangled hair away from her face with a gentle hand. 'Beautiful Libby. Look at me,' he ordered softly, and she opened her eyes and tumbled headlong into the warmth and heat of his gaze.

I love you.

The words flew into her head and out again before she had time to say them and she caught her breath.

Of course she didn't love him.

How could she possibly love him?

It was just that they'd shared something that she'd never shared with anyone before. Had she imagined the incredible connection between them? Unlike her, Andreas was obviously an experienced male—had he ever felt that with anyone else?

'Don't try and hide from me.' His voice was husky and deep and sent shivers through her body. He pulled her closer and she felt the brush of his chest hair against her sensitised nipples. 'You're shivering. Are you cold?'

Of course she was shivering. She'd just had an explosive experience that had shocked her body.

And she certainly wasn't cold.

She felt hotter than she'd ever felt in her life.

He rolled her under him again and pinned her to the ground under his powerful body. She felt incredibly vulnerable, aware of every single part of him.

Andreas gave a groan and lowered his head but before he could kiss her they heard voices approaching and Libby froze in horror.

Suddenly the dream shattered and she was horribly aware of where she was.

Lying in the grass by a lake in a public place, about to be discovered.

What was she doing?

Andreas reacted with his customary cool, rolling away from her and sliding her dress back up her arms before attempting to button his shirt.

'Half my buttons are missing,' he murmured, reaching out a lean hand and catching her chin. His eyes danced with humour. 'Do you know anything about that?'

Libby pulled away from him, her face flaming as she recalled how totally uninhibited she'd been. She stooped to retrieve her shoes, wondering what had happened to her.

How could she have done such a thing?

She, who prided herself on her self-control.

But then her self-control had never really been tested before, she reminded herself, her eyes sliding to Andreas and resting on his broad shoulders as he shrugged on his jacket, effectively disguising the fact that half the buttons were missing on his shirt.

He shot her a wicked, sexy smile that made her pulse rate bolt.

'Ready to go back to the party?'

Libby lifted a hand to her tangled blonde hair, still totally confused by her feelings. *She absolutely didn't love him.* 'I can't,' she whispered, painfully self-conscious. 'I look—'

'You look stunning,' he said quietly, stepping towards her and cupping her face in his hands.

He kissed her softly and then threaded his fingers through hers and led her back across the grass, past groups of people who were all enjoying the cool night air after the stifling heat of the ballroom.

Libby kept her face down as they walked and when they reached the terrace just outside the ballroom Andreas stopped and lifted her chin so that she was forced to look at him.

'Your guilt is written all over your face,' he murmured, his tone amused as he stroked her hair away from her flushed face. 'If it really troubles you that much, go to the ladies and redo your make-up.'

Totally shaken by what had happened and glad of an excuse to have five minutes to herself to gather her thoughts, Libby nodded and pulled away from him, hurrying inside to the ladies.

She locked herself in a cubicle and leaned against the door, her eyes tightly closed.

She didn't love him. She couldn't possibly love him.

It was just sex.

But she didn't do just sex.

She wasn't sure which was worse—the fact that she'd done something so reckless in the first place or the fact that she desperately wanted to do it again.

Oh, help!

What had she been thinking? And she knew the answer

to that, of course. *She hadn't been thinking at all.* All right, so Andreas was the sexiest man she'd ever laid eyes on but at the same time this was *her*, and she just didn't behave like that. She'd never been interested in sex outside the confines of a serious relationship.

But, then, she'd never experienced good sex before tonight, she acknowledged wryly, opening her eyes and taking a deep breath. Suddenly she was aware of what she'd been missing all her life.

So what happened now?

She wasn't stupid enough to believe that Andreas wanted anything other than a short-term relationship. She was just an interesting diversion to him.

But that just wasn't going to work for her.

She liked him. A lot.

And, given a chance, she knew that it could be more than a lot.

Shaken by the intensity of what had happened between them, she knew that it wasn't an experience that she could risk repeating. Sooner or later she'd end up being seriously hurt. She knew that she couldn't enjoy that sort of physical closeness with a man without it developing into an emotional closeness, and that was something that Andreas wouldn't want.

Neither did she, Libby reminded herself firmly. She didn't want it either.

Which meant that she had to move on and pretend that it had never happened. Yes, that was it. She just needed to pretend that it had never happened. Isn't that what people did after one-night stands? They just went their separate ways and never referred to 'it' again.

She groaned. Unfortunately, 'it' was something that she was never going to forget. And working with Andreas every day just made things doubly difficult.

She ran a hand over her face, wondering whatever could have possessed her to do something quite so stupid.

But she knew what had happened.

She'd been overwhelmed by the chemistry between them, seduced by his warmth and his breathtaking sex appeal. He had an amazing way of making her feel as though she were the only woman in the world.

As if he really cared.

In fact, she'd been so overwhelmed it would have been all too easy to convince herself that he really felt something for her.

Which was utterly ridiculous.

She sucked in a breath and gave herself a sharp talking-to.

She was becoming delusional. Seduced by the romance of the evening. She needed to go home to the familiarity of her flat before she did something stupid.

Having made the decision, she slid out of the ladies' toilets with the minimum of fuss and made her way up the stairs, walking purposefully in the hope that no one would stop her.

They didn't and within minutes she was at the front of the hotel and hailing a taxi.

She stepped into the cab with a feeling of relief, pushing away the feeling of guilt that Andreas would still be waiting for her on the terrace.

He'd probably be a bit annoyed with her at first, but he wouldn't mind that much. To him it had just been a one-night stand.

He was surrounded by women who were desperate to get their claws into him, so losing her wasn't going to matter to him, was it?

She wasn't coming back.

Andreas breathed out heavily as he acknowledged that Libby had fled.

The irony of the situation wasn't lost on him.

For all of his adult life women had pursued him relentlessly, all of them hoping to be the one to finally make him settle down.

But he'd never been even remotely tempted.

Until now.

He still couldn't quite believe what had happened down by the lake. There was something about Libby that seemed to make him lose control in public places.

He'd only known her for a month but he knew without a shadow of a doubt that Libby was the woman he wanted to spend the rest of his life with.

The trouble was, the woman he'd finally fallen in love with had just vanished into the sunset.

CHAPTER SEVEN

LIBBY arrived on the ward the following morning, relieved that she was working. At least she didn't have time to brood. And as it was a Sunday it was extremely unlikely that she'd see Andreas, which gave her another day before she had to face him.

She'd bumped into Alex at breakfast, looking decidedly the worse for wear, and he'd given her a curious look but hadn't questioned her about her mysterious disappearance the night before.

Libby gave a wry smile. Knowing her brother, he'd probably disappeared himself and hadn't even noticed her absence.

She tied her hair up, checked that her sleepless night didn't show on her face and walked onto the ward.

Poppy, the little girl with cystic fibrosis who was back on the ward yet again, greeted her cheerfully from the side ward. 'How was your party?'

Libby lifted her eyebrows. 'And how do you know about the party, young lady?'

Poppy grinned. 'I heard everyone talking about it yesterday and they said that you were going with Dr Christakos. I think you're so lucky. He's so cool.'

Remembering the fiery heat of their encounter by the lake, Libby sucked in a breath.

Not cool.

'The party was fine, thank you, Poppy,' she said, taking the little girl's temperature and nodding with satisfaction as she read the result. 'And if you carry on improving like this, you'll be back home and going to your own parties soon enough.'

Poppy's face brightened. 'Am I better?'

'Definitely better. The physiotherapist will be up soon to sort out those lungs of yours.'

Poppy groaned. 'I hate physio.'

Libby sighed and gave her a hug. 'I know you do, sweetheart, but it helps, you know it does. Where's your dad this morning?'

'Gone for breakfast in the canteen. He was starving.'

Libby pulled a face. 'Well, the food there is enough to cure anyone of hunger so he'll be back soon. Why don't you use the playroom when the physio has been?'

They encouraged the children to get up and use the playroom, rather than sitting on their beds, and Bev had lost no time in spending some of the money that they'd raised at the auction.

Poppy shifted awkwardly on the bed. 'I don't really know anyone...'

'You know me,' Libby said cheerfully, filling in her chart. 'I'll be there.'

Poppy smiled. 'Oh, well, in that case...'

Making a mental note to take Poppy to the playroom later, Libby moved on to her next little patient.

Rachel Miller was back in for some tests. The baby was sitting in her cot cooing happily and playing with a stuffed toy.

Alison smiled when she saw Libby. 'She's fine now, but Dr Christakos wanted her to have those tests and they couldn't do them when she was in a few weeks ago.'

Libby nodded. 'They shouldn't take long.' Libby leaned into the cot and pulled faces at Rachel, who chuckled happily and reached to grab her. 'She's gorgeous, Alison. You're very lucky.'

'I know.' Alison smiled proudly at her daughter. 'We wanted a baby so badly and we tried for so long to have her. I still have to pinch myself.'

Libby looked at the little girl wistfully, feeling a sick empty feeling in the pit of her stomach.

She knew all about wanting a baby badly. There were days when she positively ached for a child of her own. But she was rapidly coming to the conclusion that it was never going to happen.

Part of her envied women who happily went ahead and produced babies without the support of a partner and she was aware that it was happening more and more frequently as women made decisions about their lives without the involvement of a man.

But she wasn't like that.

She was old-fashioned enough to believe that a baby was a miracle that should be shared with someone you loved. That a baby was part of the person you loved.

Libby sighed and straightened.

She really must stop being so soppy and romantic. Real life just wasn't like that any more. People got divorced. People had babies without partners. And people had one-night stands. It was a fact of life. It was just that she didn't want it to be a fact of *her* life.

She'd always wanted so much more than that, but it seemed that love and fidelity was an endangered species.

With that thought in her head she went through to the treatment room to fetch something—and came face to face with Andreas.

Libby felt the blood drain out of her cheeks and looked round for a suitable means of escape.

'Well, hello, there. Remember me?' His voice was a lazy drawl and he planted himself firmly in front of the door so that her exit was blocked. 'We were at a ball together and then suddenly you vanished.'

And given the chance, she'd vanish again.

'I went to the ladies.'

He lifted an eyebrow. 'You spent the night there?'

She flushed. 'I don't want to talk about this now.'

'Well, I do,' he said pleasantly, and she glared at him.

'What are you doing here anyway?'

Those dark eyes mocked her. 'I work here.'

'But it's Sunday,' she muttered, screwing her fingers into her palms and trying to stop her knees trembling. She was fast discovering that it was impossible to look at him without remembering what he'd made her feel. 'I wasn't expecting to see you on a Sunday.'

In fact, she'd been banking on it.

He gave a faint smile. 'Avoiding me, Libby?'

'No.' She managed a casual shrug, wondering just how fast a heart could beat before it exploded. 'Why would you think that?'

'Well, it could be something to do with the fact that you vanished in the middle of the evening,' he said, and she looked away from him.

It had been a pretty dreadful thing to do.

Suddenly feeling guilty for the way she'd behaved, she looked at him uncertainly. 'I'm sorry if I damaged your ego.'

He studied her with brooding concentration. 'My ego is totally bombproof, *agape mou*. But I do want to know what made you run.'

Him.

Her feelings.

'I didn't run.'

'You escaped to the ladies and never returned,' he reminded her softly, a hint of a smile playing around his firm mouth. 'I assumed your name must be Cinderella and I searched everywhere for white mice and pumpkins but there was nothing in sight. Not even a stray shoe. All I could see was a cloud of dust as you vanished into the distance.'

'I didn't run. I just thought—I…' Her excuses faltered under his dark scrutiny. 'Well, I thought that was it so I might as well go home.'

Before she'd started fantasising about fairy-tale endings.

She absolutely didn't love him.

'You thought that was *it*?' He lifted a dark eyebrow. 'Excuse me?'

She tucked a strand of hair behind her ear and tried to look casual. 'We had sex, Andreas. No big deal.'

'"No big deal".' Andreas repeated her words slowly. 'So, if it was no big deal, Libby, why did you run away?'

Oh, why couldn't he just drop it?

'Look…' Libby closed her eyes briefly, wishing he wasn't quite so astute or persistent. 'It was just a one-night stand. Plenty of people have them.'

Just not her.

Andreas looked at her thoughtfully. 'You poor thing. You really are scared, aren't you?'

'Scared?' Libby stiffened defensively. 'What am I supposed to be scared of?'

Andreas shrugged. 'At a guess—letting go. Trusting someone.' He moved closer to her. 'Obviously what we shared last night scared you so much that you panicked and couldn't face me again.'

'That's not true,' she lied, and he gave a wry smile.

'Libby, you know it is true.'

'Stop making it into something it wasn't,' she said frantically. 'It was just a one-night stand. It was just sex.'

'"Just sex".' He repeated her words slowly, and his expression was suddenly serious. 'Libby, are you taking the Pill?'

She stared at him, thrown by his question. Then she shook her head.

'Right.' His voice was unbelievably gentle. 'So, if what happened between us last night was "just sex", how come neither of us thought to use contraception?'

She paled and took a step backwards.

Contraception hadn't even entered her head, either before or afterwards.

And obviously it hadn't entered his either.

Oh, help.

Andreas rubbed a hand over his dark jaw. 'The reason neither of us thought about contraception,' he said finally, his Greek accent suddenly very pronounced, 'is because it wasn't ''just sex''. It was a hell of a lot more than that, as we both know. Neither of us planned it—it just happened—but, looking back on it, it was inevitable. It's been there since the first moment we laid eyes on each other.'

Libby was still staring at him, stunned by the revelation that they hadn't used contraception.

Why hadn't it occurred to her before? She might be relatively inexperienced, but she wasn't naïve. Why hadn't she thought of contraception?

Because she hadn't been thinking about practical things. In fact, she hadn't been thinking at all. All she'd done had been to feel and react.

And now she could be pregnant.

Without thinking, she placed a hand on her abdomen. Andreas, sharp-eyed as ever, caught the movement and his eyes narrowed.

'I am truly sorry for having failed to protect you,' he said softly, sliding his hands around her face and forcing her to look at him. 'There is no excuse and I have to confess that it is the first time in my life that I've ever lost control.'

She could well believe it. Andreas Christakos was the original Mr Cool.

So what was he saying? That she was special? Different?

Did he really expect her to believe that?

Trapped by that dark gaze, Libby was severely tempted.

No, no, no!

She was doing it again.

Losing herself in the fairy-tale when she should know better.

Gentle words were just part of the standard male seduction technique, she reminded herself firmly. Andreas wasn't any different. Except perhaps that he was more skilled at it than the average male.

Any minute now he'd produce the wife or start the 'I don't do commitment' speech.

'It was my fault as much as yours,' she said finally, still unable to understand what had happened. She'd totally lost control and that had never happened to her before. She had never lost control with a man. Never felt remotely like ripping off all her clothes and making love by a lake with a couple of hundred people only metres away.

His voice was gentle. 'We need to talk about what you want to do.'

Do?

Libby looked at him, startled, and noticed that he seemed strangely tense.

'Do you want to take the morning-after pill? I could give you a prescription.'

Trying not to mind that he was so keen for her to sort the matter out, still shell-shocked by the revelation that she could be pregnant, Libby shook her head.

'I—I'll sort something out,' she mumbled evasively, totally confused by her feelings.

She was a single woman with no partner. She ought to be rushing to the chemist to get the morning-after pill.

So why were her legs glued to the spot?

Andreas frowned slightly. 'Libby—'

'I don't want to take the morning-after pill,' she said flatly, unable to be anything but honest. 'It doesn't seem right.'

Suddenly the confusion in her head cleared and her thoughts were clear.

There was absolutely no doubt at all in her mind.

If she was pregnant then she was going to keep the baby.

There was a strange look on his face that she couldn't interpret.

'There's no need to panic,' she muttered, her eyes sliding

away from his. 'I don't expect you to take any responsibility.'

Andreas frowned. 'Responsibility? Libby—'

The door opened and one of the staff nurses stuck her head round, interrupting him before he could finish his sentence.

'Dr Christakos, A and E are on the phone. It's urgent.'

Andreas gritted his teeth and strode out of the room, almost sending the nurse flying.

Libby stared after him and she was still staring into space when he returned only moments later.

'That was your brother-in-law,' he said, his mouth set in a grim line. 'There's been a nasty house fire and two children were involved. They're on their way in now but they're already struggling in A and E so he wants some help.'

Libby pulled herself together. 'Of course. I'll just tell Bev.'

She hurried off to find the ward sister and then met Andreas in the corridor and they both made their way to A and E. Andreas didn't make further reference to their conversation but she felt his eyes on her.

The department was frantically busy. The waiting room was bulging with people and the screen was flashing up a waiting time of five hours.

'And it's going to be longer than that,' Katy told them quickly, following their gaze. 'We're having a bad day down here. Thanks for your help. We thought that you could sort the children out—maybe take them straight to the ward if you prefer.'

Andreas gave a brief nod. 'We'll assess them here and then decide. What's been going on?'

'A coach overturned on one of the bridges,' Katy told him, her face drawn and tired. 'We're all struggling. And now Ambulance Control has rung about the fire. Apparently it was a nasty one. The mother jumped from the window with the baby. She's fractured both femurs and she's in a bad way, although they think the baby is fine. The father went back into the house to try and get to the other child.'

Before they could discuss the case any further they heard sirens as several ambulances pulled into the ambulance bay.

'OK, let's move!' Miraculously, Jago and one of the A and E consultants appeared and took charge. He spoke swiftly to the paramedics, conducted brief triage in the back of the ambulance and then reappeared, his expression grim. 'Katy, I want the mother and the father into Resus straight away, and fast-bleep the orthopaedic surgeons. Andreas, do you want the children on the ward or down here?'

'I'll assess them here.' Andreas stepped forward to talk to the other paramedic. 'What's the story?'

'The baby seems to be unhurt. The mother took the brunt of the fall and she was cradling the child so the little one may be all right, but she herself jumped from the bedroom window, which was quite a drop. Baby's been crying non-stop but no signs of burns. The four-year-old is a different matter. Her pyjamas caught fire and she's got nasty burns to her legs. We've given her oxygen at the scene and covered them.'

'OK—take them both through to Paediatric Resus,' Andreas ordered, and Libby hurried ahead of him to the area of A and E that had been designed specially for children.

The paramedics lifted the howling four-year-old onto the trolley and kept hold of the baby, who was also shrieking.

Charlotte, one of the A and E sisters, hurried forward. 'I'll take her while you examine the older child.'

Andreas was already by her side, talking to her gently, trying to assess the degree of damage. 'Can we weigh her quickly? Once we've done that I want to estimate the surface area of the burns and then get this child some pain relief,' he ordered quietly, and Libby did as he'd instructed. 'We need to get a line in and then we'll give her a bolus of morphine.'

Libby gathered the necessary equipment while Andreas

examined the screaming child, calculating the percentage of the body surface that had suffered burns.

'If we take her hand to be the equivalent of one per cent of her body surface area, she's suffered about ten per cent burns, most of them partial thickness,' he murmured, as he examined the little girl's legs. 'Would you agree?'

'Sounds about right.' Libby nodded, running her eyes over the burns on the child's legs.

'These blisters have ruptured and they're weeping. She's obviously feeling pain.'

'Which is a good thing,' Libby said softly, and Andreas nodded.

'Absolutely. As we both know, it's a sign that the nerve endings aren't damaged. I've checked her chest and it seems clear so there's no sign of smoke inhalation. What we have to worry about now is fluid loss.'

Libby nodded. She knew that fluid loss was proportionately greater in children than adults.

'Poor little mite. You'll want to admit her,' she said immediately. 'When you're finished here I'll call Bev and see if she can go in the side room. Melanie Parker is well enough to be on the main ward now.'

Andreas nodded. 'It would probably do her good to be mixing with the other children. OK, let's get on with this. What's her name?'

Libby checked the notes that the paramedic had left. 'Jenny.'

'Right, Jenny…' Andreas positioned himself so that he was close to the girl without actually touching her. She was still screaming hysterically. 'We are going to take that pain away.'

Jenny continued to scream for her mother and Libby exchanged worried looks with Andreas.

'Let's get on with it,' he muttered, and Libby breathed out heavily. It was horrible, seeing the child so distressed. She was sobbing now and Libby couldn't stand it a moment longer. She pulled up a chair, wrapped the child in a sterile towel and scooped her onto her lap, cuddling her close.

'There, sweetheart,' she crooned. 'Mummy will be coming in a minute. There's a good girl.'

She continued to talk soothing nonsense while Andreas searched for a vein. Libby prayed that he'd find one quickly, watching his lean, brown hands as he tapped and squeezed until he was satisfied.

He rocked back on his heels and pulled a face. 'Well, I think that looks hopeful.'

The A and E sister stepped forward. 'I'll squeeze.' She wrapped her hands around the tiny wrist and squeezed while Andreas slipped the cannula into the vein with ridiculous ease.

Libby let out a sigh of relief and Charlotte whistled in admiration.

'Nice work,' she said cheerfully, taping the cannula in place and attaching it to the bag of intravenous fluids. 'Here's that morphine you requested.'

She waved the syringe under his nose and Andreas checked it carefully before taking it from her and injecting it slowly into the tube.

'We'll start with this and she can have more in ten minutes if it hasn't done the trick.'

Jenny clung to Libby, shivering and sobbing until gradually the drug took effect and the little girl slumped in Libby's arms.

Andreas straightened and rubbed a hand over the back of his neck. 'OK, let's do a map of those burns and dress them, and then I want to pass a catheter so that we can measure her urine output.'

They worked as quickly as they could and Jenny clung to Libby, obviously seeing her as some sort of substitute mother.

Finally Andreas was satisfied that they'd done all they

could. 'We need to check that her fluid replacement is adequate. I want an output of one mil per kilogram per hour.'

Libby nodded and she and Charlotte manoeuvred the child onto the scales, recording the result in the notes.

'Right, let's get her up to the ward and make her comfortable. Keep an eye on her pulses in case her circulation is compromised. Now, how's that baby?'

'She seems fine.' While she'd been helping with Jenny, the A and E sister had put the baby safely in a cot and she was now lying there quietly. 'Do you want to check her here or on the ward?'

'I'll do it here.' Andreas unlooped the stethoscope from around his neck and walked across to the baby.

With Jenny still snuggled on her lap, Libby watched as he examined the baby thoroughly, finally picking her up and making her laugh by blowing raspberries on her stomach.

'She seems none the worse for her dramatic fall,' Andreas observed quietly, holding the child with the easy confidence of someone who was thoroughly at home with children.

Libby watched him, unable to stop herself. He was just so good with children.

It was amazing that he didn't have any himself.

But that would have meant settling down with one woman, and that clearly wasn't his style.

And he obviously wasn't that keen to be a father. After all, he'd been the one to suggest that she take the morning-after pill.

Pushing the thought away, she stood up, intending to place Jenny on the trolley so that she could dress her legs, but the little girl clung to her and whimpered pathetically.

'I'll do the dressings,' Charlotte said immediately. 'She seems to have taken to you so it seems a shame to upset her again. Keep her on your lap and I'll sort it out.'

She bustled around the room, collecting various bits and pieces, and then pushed a dressing trolley close to Libby.

With the deft efficiency of a nurse who was well used to

doing dressings, Charlotte covered the burns and made the child comfortable.

'Carry her up to the ward,' Andreas advised softly, placing a large, reassuring hand on the child's head. 'She's had just about all the trauma she can take, poor thing.'

Libby nodded and shifted the child into a more comfortable position, careful not to hurt her injured legs.

'I'll take her up, then,' she said quietly, and Andreas nodded.

'I just want to get an update on the parents and then I'll join you with this little one. It won't hurt to have her in overnight, given the fall she suffered, and we can't exactly discharge her anyway until we know what's happening with the parents.'

Libby nodded and left him to it, carrying little Jenny the short distance to the paediatric ward.

Bev was waiting for them, the room all ready, clucking with sympathy when she saw the child. 'Oh, the poor mite—how are her parents?'

Libby shook her head. 'We don't know yet. Andreas is talking to Jago now.'

Bev sighed and pulled out a chair so that Libby could sit down. 'It looks as though you're going to be occupied for the rest of the shift so I'll reallocate the rest of your patients. Luckily we're not that pushed today so it shouldn't be too difficult.'

'Thanks, Bev.' Libby cuddled Jenny closer. Like the ward sister, she knew that staying with the child was the most important thing she could do at the moment. 'What are we going to do with the baby?'

'We've got a spare cot in with Rachel,' Bev said, hooking Jenny's infusion up to a drip stand. 'I thought we'd put her in there for now.'

'Good idea.'

Libby cuddled Jenny close, talking to her quietly until she fell asleep, her soft hair brushing against Libby's cheek.

'I'm glad she's asleep.' Andreas spoke from the doorway and Libby looked up to find him leaning against the doorframe, watching them, his handsome face inscrutable. 'You look good with a child on your lap, Libby.'

She blushed and changed the subject. 'How are her parents?'

Andreas pulled a face. 'Not good. Her mother is in Theatre now—she fractured both femurs in the fall so she's going to be in hospital for a good while.'

'Poor lady.' Libby considered the implications of his words. The woman had two young children. How was she going to manage? 'Did she suffer burns?'

'Apparently not.' Andreas shook his head. 'She jumped out of the bedroom window with the baby to get away from the smoke. How is the baby, by the way?'

'Seems fine.' Libby spoke softly, careful not to wake Jenny who was still dozing, snuggled against her chest. 'Bev's made up a cot in Rachel's room and put her there for now. I suppose we'll need to find out if there are any other family members to care for her. What about the father? How's he?'

'Suffering smoke inhalation and quite severe burns to his hands where he tried to remove Jenny's pyjamas.' Andreas ran a hand through his dark hair, his expression suddenly weary. 'He certainly isn't going to be in a position to care for a baby on his own for some time.'

Libby sighed. 'Have we managed to contact any other family? Do the neighbours know of anyone?'

'The police are looking into it,' Andreas told her, his eyes resting on Jenny. 'Poor little thing. She looks exhausted.'

'It's all that crying,' Libby murmured, bending her head and dropping a light kiss on the little one's head. 'It's hardly surprising she was upset. The one person you want when you're hurt is your mummy and hers wasn't around.'

Andreas lifted his gaze. 'But she seems to have bonded with you.' His voice was deep and the look in his eyes was extremely unsettling. 'You have a very special gift with children, Libby. They love you.'

Her heart thudded in her chest and breathing was suddenly difficult. 'Better with children than adults,' she said lightly, dragging her gaze away from his. 'Children don't let you down.'

'Neither do most adults,' he responded quietly. 'You've just been unlucky. And we have a conversation to finish, Libby.'

She didn't even pretend that she didn't know what he meant.

He wanted to talk about the possibility that she could be pregnant.

But there was no way she was going to take the morning-after pill and she didn't want him to try and talk her into it.

'It's fine, Andreas,' she said softly, lifting her eyes to his. 'It's not your concern.'

He frowned. 'If you're pregnant then it's my concern.'

She blushed, slightly embarrassed by the intimacy of the discussion and desperately hoping that no one was in the corridor, listening to the conversation. She wondered briefly what had happened to her notion of discretion since she'd met Andreas. First they'd made love in the open air where anyone could have discovered them and now they were discussing the consequences in the middle of a busy hospital ward.

'I'm a modern woman,' Libby said lightly, looking away from him again. 'If it happens, rest assured that I'm not going to chase you for money.'

His gaze darkened ominously. 'Unfortunately, I'm not a modern guy,' he responded icily. 'I'm Greek and Greek men are notoriously old-fashioned about things like that. If you're pregnant, Libby, you'll be getting much more from me than money.'

Without giving her a chance to respond, he strode out of the room, leaving her staring after him.

CHAPTER EIGHT

LIBBY managed to avoid Andreas for the rest of the shift by staying with Jenny.

When the night staff arrived she was still in the little girl's room, cuddling her, talking softly to her, making her feel more secure in her strange surroundings. There seemed no hope that she'd be able to see either of her parents before the morning.

Her mother was still in Theatre and her father was being treated for smoke inhalation.

'The neighbour thinks that there's an aunt living nearby,' Bev told her, 'but no one has any idea how to contact her. We'll just have to wait for one of the parents to tell us. In the meantime, we'll keep the baby overnight. Andreas seems keen to keep an eye on her anyway, given the seriousness of the fall.'

'I can't believe she survived it,' Libby murmured softly, careful not to wake Jenny, who was dozing quietly.

'Well, the mother obviously took the brunt of the impact.' Bev looked at the little girl lying on the bed. 'She seems more peaceful. Has she had more morphine?'

Libby nodded. 'It will be good when she can see one of her parents. She needs the reassurance.'

Bev nodded. 'Well, hopefully we'll manage something tomorrow. We can always carry her up to them if necessary.' Her eyes narrowed as she looked at Libby. 'You look exhausted. You should have requested the day off today. How late did you get to bed?'

Not that late, Libby reflected. But she'd been awake for most of the night thinking about Andreas. *Dreaming about fairy-tales and happy endings.*

'I'm fine.'

'What you need is some proper time off. You've got a few days' leave due. I want you to take them.'

Libby looked at her. 'Bev, we're far too busy for me to take leave.'

Bev shrugged. 'You're knackered, Lib. You're no use to me like this. You've been working double shifts for as long as I can remember and you need a rest. I'll ring the agency and see if I can get someone for the week after next.'

Libby frowned. 'Holiday leave…'

'Yes, holiday leave,' Bev said firmly. 'You've got five days. For goodness' sake, go away somewhere.'

Libby looked at her blankly. She didn't really want to go anywhere. She didn't have the energy. If she wasn't going to work, all she really wanted to do was go to bed and sleep for ever.

'I'll see how things are,' she said vaguely, thinking that it might actually be nice to have a few days at home, doing nothing. She could lie in bed in the mornings and meet Katy for lunch. 'If you're sure, that is.'

'I'm sure,' Bev said firmly, breaking off as Andreas strolled into the room.

Libby felt her stomach turn over. He was so good-looking he took her breath away and she was starting to have really, really foolish thoughts.

Thoughts about being pregnant and him insisting on marrying her.

Ridiculous!

She closed her eyes briefly, horrified by the way her mind was working.

What was the matter with her? She was thinking like someone who wasn't thoroughly disillusioned with men.

A holiday was definitely a good idea. It would mean putting space between her and Andreas. And she needed that space.

Her mind seemed to have a will of its own and she was

starting to believe that Andreas might be different from all the other men she'd ever met.

She definitely needed a holiday.

Libby picked up her bag and left the ward, thinking longingly of her bed.

She just hoped that tonight she'd sleep.

Last night she hadn't managed to do anything except think of Andreas. She'd lain in the darkness, reliving every incredible second of their encounter by the lake. The memory had been so vivid that she'd almost been able to smell the damp grass and feel the cool night air on her skin. Her body had tingled with the memory of his touch and she could still hear the rough, masculine timbre of his voice as he'd spoken to her in Greek. She hadn't been able to understand a word that he'd said but it had been an unbelievably erotic experience and she couldn't get it out of her mind.

Damn.

Running a hand over her flushed face, she tried to pull herself together. It had just been sex, for crying out loud. Just sex, and she'd done it before.

But it had never been like that.

With Andreas it had been a totally different experience and if she was ever going to survive, she had to avoid him. And what better way to avoid him than by taking a holiday?

She could spend the time reminding herself that all men were rats.

Andreas stared at the notes in front of him without seeing them. For the third day running Libby had been in Jenny's room for almost the entire shift, not even coming out for lunch. The little girl was very clingy and she'd obviously bonded with Libby, but all the same it was obvious to him that she was anxious to avoid any further conversation with him and he knew why.

The chemistry between them was so overwhelming that

he found it quite unnerving himself. He'd never felt this way about a woman before and he knew that she was experiencing the same emotions.

The challenge was going to be getting her to admit it.

Libby was terrified of being hurt. She found it impossible to trust men and she was incredibly wary and cautious.

He needed to prove to her that he could be trusted but he couldn't do that unless she agreed to spend some time with him. But judging from the way she'd been avoiding him since that night, the chances of her agreeing to that were remote.

He leaned back in his chair and stretched his long legs out in front of him, frowning thoughtfully.

And then he remembered the date.

She still owed him a date.

A slow smile crossed his handsome face as he remembered the conversation he'd overheard between her and the ward sister.

No one had ever stipulated exactly what constituted the date that had been auctioned.

And suddenly he knew exactly what that date was going to be.

A week later Jenny was improving rapidly and spending much of the time in the playroom with Polly, who had taken on a surrogate mother role.

Jenny's parents were still in hospital and her baby sister had been staying with an aunt who lived locally.

The ward had quietened down slightly, Bev had found an agency nurse who'd agreed to work for the rest of the month and Libby was exhausted.

The strain of trying to avoid Andreas was making her jumpy and she wasn't getting any sleep thanks to that one incredible night she'd spent with him. She was totally unable to forget the way he'd made her feel.

She was thoroughly relieved that Bev had insisted she

take leave. At least she wouldn't have to peep round corners to check that there was no sign of Andreas. She vowed to get plenty of exercise in the hope that it would make her sleep.

Suddenly she couldn't wait for her shift to end.

She went through the motions of doing her job and at lunchtime Bev bustled up to her.

'You look absolutely wiped out.' The ward sister shook her head disapprovingly. 'Go home.'

'I can't go yet. I haven't finished my shift.'

Bev gave her a gentle push. 'Just go. Now. And if I see you back on this ward before next week, you're fired.'

Libby gave a weak smile. She couldn't actually believe she had a whole week off. 'You can't fire me. I'm your slave labour.'

Bev didn't laugh. 'You've lost your sparkle and bubble,' she said quietly. 'You've been working too hard, Lib. Have a rest.'

Libby didn't say anything. It was true that she was tired, but the truth was her sparkle had gone because she was so disappointed about Andreas. She'd really believed that he was interested in her, but evidently she'd been wrong again.

Apart from that one conversation the morning after, he'd made no attempt to see her since the ball.

All right, so she'd been avoiding him, but he hadn't been that difficult to avoid.

Wondering whether he would even notice that she wasn't around, she went to her locker, retrieved her bag and made her way to the car park, feeling flat and miserable.

A low black sports car pulled up next to her and she sucked in a breath.

Andreas.

He leaned across to open the passenger door, his expression serious. 'Get in, Libby.'

She stared at him blankly. 'Why? Where are we going?'

'Just get in.'

Something about the urgency in his tone prevented her from arguing and she slid into the passenger seat, glancing at him in alarm as he sped away before she'd even finished fastening her seat belt.

'What's happening? Is something wrong?' Suddenly she felt cold fingers of panic touch her spine. 'Is it Katy? Or Alex?'

He covered her hand briefly with his. 'They're both fine. And nothing's wrong.'

'So why are you picking me up? It's not even lunchtime.' She looked at him in confusion. 'And what's the urgency?'

He glanced at the clock and muttered something in Greek. 'We are going to be late.'

'Late for what?'

But he wouldn't answer her. He just stared at the road and drove as quickly as safety allowed, weaving his way through the London traffic until he hit the motorway that led out of town.

'Andreas.' Libby cleared her throat and tried again. 'Where are we going?'

He gave her a sideways glance. 'We're going on that date you owe me.'

Date?

He flicked the indicator and took the exit road that led to the airport and she lifted a hand to her aching head, totally confused.

'What date? Why are we at the airport?'

Andreas pulled up outside the terminal building and shifted in his seat so that he was facing her.

'You still owe me that date, Libby,' he said softly, lifting a hand to cup her face. 'I'm claiming it now. You've got a week off. You're spending it with me.'

She opened her mouth to speak but he was already out of the car, handing his keys to a man in a uniform and removing two bags from the boot.

Libby recognised one of the bags as hers.

She leapt out of the car, waiting while he paid the man and signalled for a porter.

'You packed a bag for me?' She stared at him incredulously and he shrugged.

'Not exactly. I had some help. Katy told me she owed you a suitcase full of clothes.'

Katy.

Libby groaned. 'I switched the contents of her suitcase when she went abroad with Jago. Katy always insisted on dressing really conservatively to hide her looks so Alex and I gave her a completely new wardrobe. She didn't know until she arrived in Spain and unpacked.'

Andreas laughed. 'Well, it seems as though you're not the only sister capable of being devious. And now we need to hurry or we'll miss our flight.'

Libby ran her tongue over dry lips. 'Andreas, I can't just go away with you.'

'Why not?'

Because she didn't trust him.

Because she was trying to put some distance between them and she couldn't possibly do that if they were together all week.

She opened her mouth to voice another protest but he was already striding towards the terminal building and she was forced to run to catch up with him.

'All right, if you want a date, I'll go on a date with you, but this is ridiculous.' She was half running, half walking, but he didn't slow his pace.

'Why is it ridiculous?' He shot her a smile and walked up to the check-in desk. 'I always told you that my idea of a date wasn't pizza. You just never asked what my idea of a date was. Well, this is it. We're going to spend some time together, Libby. No more avoiding me. No more avoiding what we have together.'

She stared at him as he handed over the passports and

checked in, infuriated that he wasn't even giving her a chance to speak.

'We don't have anything together,' she said in a low voice, blushing slightly as the girl behind the desk glanced curiously between the two of them. 'It was just—'

'If you're about to tell me that it was "just sex",' Andreas interrupted, 'then I'd better warn you that the next time you say that I'm going to drag you behind the nearest pillar and prove you wrong. We both know that it wasn't "just sex", Libby, so stop saying things you don't mean.'

He tucked the passports into his jacket and walked towards the international departures area.

Her breathing was rapid and she felt totally out of control.

'At least tell me where we're going,' she asked a little later.

He turned with a smile. 'We're going to Greece, *agape mou*. I'm taking you to my home.'

Greece?

'But where will we stay? What will we—?'

'Stop worrying.' He stepped up to her and covered her lips with his fingers to stop her talking. 'You're not in control any more. I am. This is *my* date, Libby.'

With that Andreas bent his head and kissed her gently, smiling when she gave a start and backed away.

She glared at him. 'This isn't a date. It's kidnap. I could scream.'

His smiled widened. 'If you scream, I'm going to kiss you senseless in front of an audience. Knowing what usually happens when we touch each other, are you willing to risk that, Libby?'

Her heart thudded against her chest. There was no way she wanted him to kiss her again. It was much too disturbing. Strange things happened when he kissed her. Her body burned and her brain ceased to be capable of logical thought.

So instead of screaming she just sighed and pretended to look bored. 'A week is a long time with someone you don't really know, Andreas. What happens when you find that you don't enjoy my company?'

He laughed. 'Libby, we both know that we're crazy about each other. It's just that you're afraid to admit it.'

Crazy about each other...

Libby swallowed hard. 'And you think I'll admit it if I'm with you all week? Are all Greek men as arrogant as you?'

Was he really saying he was crazy about her?

He nodded, giving her a gentle push as they boarded the aircraft. 'We're an arrogant, chauvinistic race who know how to keep a woman in her place,' he teased. 'Now sit down and shut up. And preferably get some sleep. You're exhausted.'

'And whose fault is that?' Libby muttered darkly, fastening her seat belt and wriggling further into her seat.

'You're saying that I'm the reason you're tired?'

His deep voice was right next to her ear and her body heated. He sounded so sexy. Oh, for goodness' sake. So the guy had a sexy voice. So what? She was being utterly pathetic.

She tried to shift further away from him but there was nowhere to go. 'I'm tired because I've been working hard,' she said sweetly, and he gave a knowing smile that infuriated her.

'Of course you are. So, sleep, Libby.'

Libby closed her eyes tightly. She had absolutely no hope of sleeping, but at least if she closed her eyes she couldn't see those dark eyes and that sexy mouth. She needed some rest if she was going to resist him.

And she was going to resist him.

No problem.

Andreas shook his head as the stewardess offered him more coffee. They'd been flying for three and a half hours and Libby had been asleep the whole time. At some point her

head had flopped onto his shoulder and he'd turned slightly
so that he could cuddle her closer and make her comfortable.

He was worried about how tired she looked.

Her cheeks were pale and there were shadows visible beneath her closed lashes. He vowed to make sure that she
had plenty of rest when they reached their destination.

He still couldn't quite believe that he'd managed to pull
it off. He'd hoped that by picking her up straight from work
with no warning she wouldn't have time to think up excuses.
And it had worked. With a great deal of help from Katy and
Bev.

So now he had a week alone with her.

One week to try and persuade her how right they were
for each other.

Libby woke feeling warm and safe and then she realised
that the person she was cuddling was Andreas and she sat
bolt upright, pink with embarrassment.

Bother.

Andreas made no comment. Instead, he shifted his shoulder slightly and reached across to look out of the window.

'Look at that,' he said softly. 'Isn't it fantastic?'

Still foggy-headed from sleep, Libby turned her head to
look out of the tiny window and gave a gasp of delight.

Beneath them stretched perfect blue sea, twinkling in the
sunlight as though someone had casually tossed a handful
of diamonds into the waves. Tiny boats were just visible
and she could see several pretty islands with sandy coves

'It's beautiful.'

'It's Greece.' Andreas smiled with satisfaction as he settled back in his seat. 'Still angry that I kidnapped you?'

Libby couldn't take her eyes off the sea. She wanted to
dive straight in and feel the cool water on her exhausted
body. 'I can think of worse places to be held hostage.'

'The only thing holding you hostage is your inability to

trust anyone,' Andreas replied calmly. 'I'm glad you slept. Our journey isn't finished yet.'

Despite her qualms about spending the week with him, she felt suddenly excited.

Why shouldn't she enjoy a holiday?

She could keep Andreas at a distance here as easily as she could on the ward.

'Where exactly are we going?'

'Crete. My home.'

A car was waiting for them when they landed and Libby stared in awe at the scenery that flashed passed.

'It's beautiful. How can you bear to leave it?'

He smiled. 'The lure of British and American healthcare.'

'Well, I think you're mad. If this was my home I'd never leave it.' Libby gave an enormous yawn and settled back in her seat. 'Are we staying in your house?'

Andreas grabbed the bags and shook his head. 'Yes. Although none of the rest of the family will be there. My mother is visiting my cousin who's just had a baby and my uncles spend most of their time in Athens now.'

Libby shot him a wary glance. Would it be just the two of them?

Her heart lurched slightly but before she had a chance to question him further the driver had turned off the road and was driving down what was little more than a dusty track that led towards the beach.

Libby craned her neck curiously, wondering where they were going. Surely there couldn't be a house here? Nothing was visible from the road.

And then the car turned a corner and she gasped.

A beautiful whitewashed villa nestled at one end of a beautiful bay, the sand stretching away from it to form a perfect crescent.

It was the most idyllic spot she'd ever seen and she turned to Andreas in amazement.

'This is your home?'

'I was brought up here,' he told her, nodding to the driver as he retrieved the bags from the boot of the car. 'But we spent a great deal of time in Athens, too. My father had business interests there. He hated leaving his family behind so we had a home there as well.'

'You're lucky,' Libby said wistfully, and he looked at her keenly.

'Did your father travel a lot?'

Libby tensed. 'Yes, but we were all very grateful for that. Things weren't too great when he was around.'

Wanting to escape from the memories that he'd aroused, she slipped off her shoes and sprinted down to the sand, sighing with pleasure as she felt the warm softness ooze between her toes.

'You're a child, Elizabeth,' Andreas said with a laugh from behind her, and she shrugged, staring out across the sparkling sea to the orange sun that was starting to dip behind the mountains.

'I don't know about that,' she said softly, 'but I do know that if you were brought up here then you were very lucky.'

She'd heard the affection in his voice when he'd spoken of his parents and suddenly she envied him his childhood. Her own had been full of rows and totally lacking in parental affection.

Would she have been different if she'd had his family background?

Would she have found it easier to trust people?

'I was lucky,' he agreed. 'I had a secure, loving family around me when I was a child and I suppose that's why I don't find it hard to trust people. Unlike you. I know that you've been surrounded by faithless men all your life, but it's time to realise that they aren't the only sort.'

Her breathing quickened.

It would have been so easy to believe him. So easy...

And so foolish.

She gave a wry smile and kicked at the sand with her bare feet. 'So…' she lifted her head and gave him a bright smile '…are you going to show me your house?'

He lifted a hand and touched her face gently. 'You are the mistress of avoidance, do you know that?'

She gave a careless shrug. 'I don't see the point in dwelling on the past.'

'If it's affecting the future, there's a point,' he said quietly, taking her hand and pulling her back towards the villa. 'But we'll talk about that another time. Come on. Let's get settled in.'

She followed him inside, almost drooling with pleasure as she saw the interior. It was decorated in a mixture of white and cool blues so that the overall impression was that it was just a continuation of the ocean.

'I know you're tired so I'll show you straight to your bedroom,' Andreas said roughly, and she looked at him cautiously.

She hadn't given any thought to the sleeping arrangements. 'Andreas—'

'Sleep, Libby,' he said gently, 'and then we'll talk.'

Suddenly realising just how exhausted she was, she followed him into a bedroom, smiling with pleasure when she saw the bathroom. It was the last word in luxury.

'I can't believe you brought me here. I ought to be fighting with you,' she murmured, reaching forward and flicking on the taps, 'but frankly I'm too exhausted.'

'Thank goodness for that.' Andreas gave a wry smile and deposited her suitcase on the floor. 'I'll leave you to it. My bedroom is directly opposite if you need anything.'

She stiffened. 'I won't need anything.'

His smile widened and she sucked in a breath, uncomfortably aware that they seemed to be alone in this villa. Alone for the first time in their relationship.

But he didn't seem inclined to take advantage of that fact. Instead, he flicked her cheek gently with a strong finger and left the room without a backward glance, closing the door behind him.

She stared after him, telling herself firmly that she wasn't disappointed.

He'd left her to have a bath and sleep alone in that gorgeous huge bed with the gauzy cream drapes.

And that was exactly what she wanted.

Wasn't it?

Two days later Libby wondered how she was ever going to bring herself to leave the island.

She'd spent most of her time cooling down in the sea or in the fantastic azure blue pool that overlooked the beach. When she wasn't swimming she slept, and every time she awoke there seemed to be more food waiting for her. Greek salads, dips, plump olives and regional specialities that made her mouth water.

Andreas had explained on the first day that one of the families from the neighbouring village looked after the villa and kept an eye on his mother when she was staying there. They were also responsible for delivering vast quantities of delicious food every day.

'You're trying to fatten me up,' she groaned, leaning back in her chair after a spectacular lunch during which she'd eaten far too much for comfort.

Andreas poured her some more water and she tried not to notice how good he looked in his polo shirt. The fabric hugged the powerful muscles of his shoulders and his arms were tanned and strong.

He was an incredibly good-looking man and she didn't really understand why he was bothering with her.

'It's good to see you eating, rather than picking at your food the way you did the night of the ball.'

As usual, any reference to the ball brought a sudden rush of colour to Libby's cheeks. She couldn't prevent herself from glancing across at him, and instantly regretted it. His dark eyes locked onto hers and she felt heat flare deep in her pelvis.

Terrified of the strength of her reaction, she stood up abruptly, her chair scraping on the ground. 'It's hot. I'm going to cool off in the pool—'

Strong fingers closed around her wrist and anchored her to the spot. 'You shouldn't exercise when you've just eaten, *agape mou*. And it's time to stop avoiding me. You've rested and the colour has returned to your cheeks. No more running.'

'I'm not running.' She stood, breathing rapidly, trapped by his relentless grip and by the look in his eyes.

'Libby, you've been running since the night I bought you at that auction.' He pulled her closer and she couldn't have resisted even if she'd wanted to. 'It's time you and I communicated.'

She watched, breathless, as his head lowered, transfixed by the inevitability of that kiss. For endless, infuriating seconds his mouth hovered above hers, close enough to set her whole body on fire with anticipation but not close enough to satisfy the raging hunger building inside her.

His eyes were half-closed as he looked down at her, and a hint of a smile hovered on his incredibly sexy mouth. Finally he lowered his head and his mouth brushed against hers, sending shock waves of excitement through her quivering body.

His hands slid up to her face, cradling it firmly, while his tongue traced the seam of her lips and dipped inside. Her lips parted under the pressure of his and she kissed him back, her tongue responding to the demands of his, her body arching against the solid muscle of his powerful body.

He kissed her until her entire body was throbbing with sensation and when he finally lifted his head she stared up at him, dazed.

With considerable effort she found her voice. 'I—I thought you wanted to talk.'

He gave a slow smile and touched her damp, swollen lips with the tips of his fingers. 'I didn't say talk, *agape mou*. I said communicate.'

She gazed at him, heart thumping, hypnotised by the raw passion she saw in his eyes. 'But—'

'We're using body language,' he said huskily, his mouth lowering to hers again.

She gave a tiny sob as he licked her lips suggestively. 'Body language?'

He gave a slow smile that ignited a burning heat deep inside her. 'It's the only way I can be sure that you're telling the truth. When you use words, you say things you don't mean.'

His mouth was still so close to hers she couldn't concentrate. 'Such as?'

'Such as "I'm not interested, Andreas", or "It was just sex, Andreas". Your mouth says one thing and your body says another,' he murmured. 'So for now speaking is banned.'

Libby discovered that she actually didn't want to speak. The gentle, relentless kissing was driving her slowly crazy. She lifted her arms and wrapped them round the strong column of his neck, dragging his head down to hers again.

This time his kiss was hard and demanding, his mouth possessing every inch of hers and his arms hauling her against him. She felt the solid thrust of his erection pressing through her thin shorts and tried to get closer still, frustrated by the barrier created by the clothes they were wearing.

She lifted her hands and slid them under his shirt, groaning as she felt the warmth of his skin and the smooth swell of his muscles under her searching fingers.

His hands followed suit, lifting her tiny strap top, breaking their kiss for only a fraction of a second as he slid it over her head and let it fall onto the sun-baked terrace. Her shorts followed, and then her bra and soon she was standing in only the tiny bikini bottom that she'd worn on the beach earlier.

The slide of his hands over her bare flesh made her shiver in anticipation and she forgot her plans to resist him. Resistance just wasn't an option.

Without lifting his mouth from hers, he lifted her easily in his arms and walked the short distance to the bedroom, kicking the door shut behind him and laying her down on the middle of the bed.

Breathing rapidly, his dark eyes blazing with a sexual need that thrilled her, he yanked off his shirt and came down on top of her, kissing her again until she was writhing and sobbing beneath him.

His hands slid smoothly over her heated flesh, removing the final barrier, and finally she was naked, spread beneath him on the cool, white sheets.

Breathing harshly, he bent his head and teased her nipple, flicking gently with his tongue and then drawing her into the heat of his mouth. Tortured by an almost intolerable excitement, she gasped and stretched her arms above her head, writhing frantically in an attempt to free her body of the sexual need that threatened to consume her.

Refusing to give her the release she craved, he continued to torment her, his strong hand stroking her stomach lightly as he used his mouth on her breasts.

She shifted her hips, aware of his hand resting on her stomach and wanting it lower…

Finally, finally when she thought she was going to explode with frustration he moved his hand and found the moist, warm centre of her longing.

Feeling him touching her so intimately, she lowered her arms and slid them down his smooth, muscled back, pushing impatiently at his shorts, wanting him naked.

With a smooth movement he dispensed with the rest of his clothes and she gasped in anticipation as he moved above her.

'Look at me, Libby.' His hoarse command penetrated her dazed brain and her eyes locked onto his, registering the raw need she saw there.

The eye contact just increased the closeness and intimacy of what they were sharing and when she felt him, hard and strong against the damp heat of her femininity, she wrapped her arms around his neck, feeling him with every centimetre of her quivering body.

He entered her with a smooth, demanding thrust that left her in no doubt of just how much he wanted her and she lifted her hips, encouraging him to thrust deeper still, until there was no knowing where he ended and she began.

He possessed her fully, mind and body, his eyes burning into hers as he thrust in a pagan rhythm that had her gasping and digging her nails into the powerful muscles of his shoulders.

It was the ultimate in sexual excitement, a connection so strong that she felt as though they'd be joined for ever, and she wrapped her legs around him, rocking, giving as much as he took.

Neither of them spoke, but the air was filled with the sensual sounds of their love-making. A soft gasp, a harsh groan and ragged, uneven breathing as his body increased the rhythm, creating an agony of excitement that propelled her towards completion.

She couldn't look away from him. Even when her body exploded in a shattering climax that seemed endless, her eyes were locked on his, drawing him in, feeling him deep inside her both physically and mentally.

And even then he didn't release her. He just slowed the pace, thrusting deeply, building the heat again until she was writhing against him, desperate for the faster, pounding rhythm that would propel her upwards again, towards the mindless ecstasy that she craved.

Finally, when she thought she couldn't stand the sexual torment any longer, he shifted his weight, still staring deep into her eyes as he gave them both the exquisite satisfaction that their bodies demanded.

This time when she peaked she felt his body shudder within hers and felt the pulsing strength of him deep inside her. Her fingers tightened on his arms and she cried out his name, clinging to him in desperation as she tumbled head-long into paradise.

Gradually their breathing slowed and he rolled onto his back, holding her firmly against him, giving her no opportunity to distance herself.

She lay still in his arms, shocked by the explosion of pleasure that had rocked her entire body. Then she turned and gave him a weak smile. 'I thought you said that you shouldn't exercise when you've just eaten?'

He bent his head and kissed her. 'That,' he said slowly, 'depends on the exercise.'

Libby stayed with her head on his chest, feeling the roughness of his body hair against her cheek and the steady thud of his heart. His wonderfully male smell teased her nostrils and she closed her eyes, not wanting the moment to end.

It just felt so perfect.

But it wasn't. Nothing could be that perfect.

'I better get some clothes on—'

'No. This time you're not going anywhere.' He rolled her underneath him and stroked her damp hair away from her face. 'Having communicated honestly through body language, this is the part where you speak and admit that you have feelings for me.'

Achingly aware of the weight of his body touching every part of her, she caught her breath. 'Feelings?'

'That's right.' He gave a lazy smile and shifted slightly.

'What makes you think I have feelings?' She gasped as she felt him against her. 'It was just sex, Andreas.'

He chuckled and bent his head to kiss her again. 'Ah.

Back to "just sex" again. Tell me, Lib, how many times have you had sex like that before?'

'Oh, you know—once or twice…' She licked dry lips and tried to look casual but it was pretty hard because he was still lying on top of her and she could feel the hard muscle of his thigh wedged against hers.

He rested his forehead against hers, intensifying the contact between them. 'You're lying, *agape mou*. You've never had sex like that before.'

'You are so arrogant—'

'And the reason I know that,' he said, ignoring her interruption, 'is because I haven't either. Something happens between you and I, Libby, and it's special. Unique to us. Just ours.'

Just ours.

He was doing it again. Making it sound special.

She struggled to catch her breath. 'That's rubbish.'

'Is it?' He shifted slightly so that not one single inch of her body was left untouched by his. 'If it's rubbish, why did you run out on me the night of the ball?'

'The evening was over.' The hair on Andreas's chest teased her sensitised nipples and she struggled to concentrate as her body responded to the lightest of touches.

'You always desert your partner without saying goodbye?' He moved against her and she gasped, realising that he knew exactly what he was doing. 'No, Libby. You ran that night because what we shared was so frighteningly good—so intense—that you were scared witless. You panicked.'

She was writhing under him now, her body arching in an effort to ease the intolerable ache in her pelvis.

'Andreas…'

He gave a low growl and raked a hand through her blonde hair. 'Tell me how you *feel*, Libby. *Tell me.*'

She stared up at him, lost in the expression in his dark

eyes, her whole body feverish and quivering. She just felt so *hot*. 'I want you…'

He gave a groan of frustration and bent his head to capture her mouth. 'Admit that it's not just sex.'

Desperate for him, she gasped and arched against him. 'Andreas, please…'

'No.' His voice was a low growl. 'Not until you admit the way you feel.'

Libby whimpered. 'Do you want me to hit you?'

'Admit it.'

'Andreas…'

'I love you, Libby.' He spoke the words softly and her breathing and heart stopped simultaneously.

He loved her?

Afraid she'd misheard him, she lay utterly still and he gave a sigh and shifted slightly so that he could look at her.

'Did you hear me?'

She nodded slowly and he gave a wry smile.

'So this is the point when you tell me that you love me, too.'

Libby felt a rush of panic. *She didn't love him.* She didn't want to love him. It was asking for trouble. He'd hurt her…

'It's just sex, Andreas. Good sex, admittedly, but just sex.'

He gave a frustrated grunt. 'You're lying and if I have to pin you to this bed for the rest of your life I'm going to make you admit the truth.' His dark eyes were unbelievably gentle. 'The sex is good because we love each other, Libby. Why don't you just admit that you've never felt this way about a man before and that you're scared?'

Libby's heart was thumping so hard she could hardly breathe. 'All right. I've never felt like this about a man before and I'm scared,' she parroted, and he sighed.

'Relationships don't have to go wrong, Libby. I know you've seen some bad examples, but that doesn't mean that there aren't good examples out there, too. My parents were happily married for forty years. Why won't you just trust me?'

She bit her lip. 'Because it's been too quick, too good to be true, and because I don't believe that fairy-tales always have happy endings,'

'Then you'd better prepare yourself for a shock,' he said softly, lowering his head to kiss her gently, 'because this particular fairy-tale is going to have the best ending you can possibly imagine.'

CHAPTER NINE

ANDREAS sat on the shaded terrace and sipped his coffee.

It was already midmorning and there was no sign of Libby. But remembering just how little sleep he'd allowed her the night before, he decided that it was hardly surprising.

By contrast, he'd been up since dawn, wading through the mountains of family paperwork that always accumulated in his absence.

He'd just signed the last of the papers when he glanced up and saw her standing in the doorway that led to the terrace, wearing a pair of white shorts and a light blue top.

His eyes dropped to her legs and his body reacted in a surge of sexual hunger that took him by surprise. They'd made love for most of yesterday and all of last night and he still wanted her.

But she still hadn't said that she loved him.

'I'm sorry I slept so late.' She looked extremely self-conscious and Andreas sucked in a breath and ditched the papers he'd been reading, his concentration gone.

There was only one thing he thought of when he looked at Libby, and it certainly wasn't business.

'I'm glad you slept well.' His voice sounded husky and he wondered if she had any idea of the effect she had on him. Probably not or she wouldn't have worn those shorts. 'Come here.'

She walked towards him and he dragged her onto his lap, stroking her hair away from her face and kissing her urgently.

'I love you.' He groaned the words against her mouth and she pulled away, her blue eyes wary and more than a little frightened.

'Stop saying that.'

'It's the truth. And you love me, too.'

Perhaps if he said the words often enough, eventually she'd find the courage to say them herself.

She slid off his lap and he saw the confusion in her eyes. 'Andreas…'

'Trust me, Libby.'

'Let's go to the beach.'

Andreas suppressed a sigh, wondering what it would take to break through the wall of self-protection that she'd built around herself.

They spent the days swimming and talking and making love, and the time passed too quickly for Libby. She could have stayed there for ever, locked in the tiny world they'd created, safe from outside influences.

There was something magical about the villa and the bay.

Something unreal.

It felt so far away from their real lives.

It was as if anything could happen here, but once they returned home life would just return to normal.

She was lying on a sun lounger with her eyes closed, trying to catch up on some lost sleep, when she felt the familiar tug in her stomach.

Her heart lurched.

Not wanting to believe the messages that her body was sending, she rushed to her room to discover that her period had started.

She'd been so wrapped up in the emotional high of being with Andreas that she'd temporarily forgotten that she might be pregnant.

Swamped by a feeling of desolation that she couldn't comprehend, she went to the bathroom and burst into tears, sobbing against the tiled wall until her head started to ache.

She tried to analyse why she was crying but her head was pounding too hard to allow her access to her thoughts.

Surely she should have been relieved that she wasn't pregnant?

Why did she feel so utterly devastated?

She didn't even know that Andreas had followed her until she felt herself gathered against his hard chest.

For several minutes she just sobbed without speaking and then she took the tissue he handed her and blew her nose hard.

'Why are you crying?'

She shook her head and scrunched the tissue into a ball, too upset to speak.

'Libby.' His tone was urgent and he put her away from him and cupped her face in his hands, forcing her to look at him. 'Tell me.'

'It's nothing,' she hiccoughed. 'It's my problem, not yours.'

His face darkened and his fingers bit into her scalp. 'If this is what I think it is, then it's very much my problem, too. Only actually I don't see it as a problem.'

She closed her eyes and shook her head. He'd misunderstood, and who could blame him? 'Just drop it Andreas— please…'

She needed some time on her own. Time to pull herself together. She was being ridiculous.

'I thought I'd made it clear that I'm very traditional when it comes to certain things,' he said softly, showing no signs of releasing her. 'Tell me why you're crying, because if you're afraid that I won't want you now you're pregnant, you couldn't be more wrong.'

Libby pulled away from him and scrubbed the palm of her hand over her cheeks to get rid of the tears.

'I'm not crying because I'm pregnant,' she gulped finally, her voice jumpy from too much crying. 'I'm crying because I'm *not* pregnant. OK?'

She gave a massive sniff, aware that Andreas was unusually still.

'You're *not* pregnant?'

Just hearing the words upset her again and her face crumpled. 'That's right—I'm *not* pregnant. And now will you leave me alone?'

She turned away from him but he reached out and grabbed her, hauling her round so that she was facing him, his fingers biting into her upper arms.

'If you're not pregnant, Libby, why are you crying?'

She tried to glare at him but instead her face crumpled again and she gave another sob. 'Because I wanted to be pregnant, you dummy! I *wanted* your baby.' She was vaguely aware that she was shouting but she didn't even care. 'Which just goes to show how stupid I can be.'

Andreas stared at her, his dark gaze strangely intent. 'And why did you want my baby, Libby?' His voice was hoarse and she tried to focus on him through watery eyes.

'I don't know,' she muttered, and his fingers tightened on her arms.

'Yes, you do. Why, Libby?'

She hiccoughed slightly. 'Because you're very good-looking and I thought we'd make cute babies?'

He lifted an eyebrow and his firm mouth quirked slightly. 'So you selected me as a prime example of male genetic perfection?'

'Maybe.'

He looked at her. 'Come on, Libby,' he urged softly, 'be honest with me. Be honest with yourself for once.'

Heart racing, she spread her hands and glared at him. 'All right, I love you,' she shouted. 'I love you heaps and tons. And it's terrifying because I know that it won't last because it never does. And finding out that I'm not pregnant is horrible. I didn't even know I wanted to be pregnant until five minutes ago when I found out that I wasn't. How illogical is that?'

'It's the best news I've ever had,' he groaned, dragging

her against him. 'I was beginning to think that I'd never get you to admit how you feel.'

Libby stared up at him, her lower lip wobbling. 'I wanted to be pregnant.'

He gave a slow smile. 'I'll make you pregnant,' he promised, lowering his head to kiss her. 'As many times as you like. I adore children, you know that. I'd given up ever finding a woman who felt the same way.'

Libby blinked, still very unsure.

Andreas wanted children?

He wanted to have children with *her*?

'But you wanted me to take the morning-after pill.'

Andreas curved a strong hand round her cheek, staring down into her eyes as he shook his head. 'No. That was the last thing I wanted.'

She stared at him, wide-eyed. 'So why did you suggest it?'

'Because you were panicking enough at the thought of us being a couple, without me admitting how much I wanted to have children with you,' Andreas said quietly. 'If you had wanted to take the pill, I would have supported you, but I was immensely relieved that you decided not to.'

She was still reeling from the shock of finally admitting that she was in love with him. She'd been fighting it for so long she hadn't even admitted it to herself.

She looked at him, her heart thudding. 'So is this the bit where we live happily ever after?'

'I think it probably is,' he agreed, stroking the tears away from her cheek with gentle fingers, 'although the final scene isn't usually played out in a bathroom with the bride-to-be looking traumatised. Wash your face or I'll have to tell our children that I proposed to their mother when she had a red nose.'

She sniffed. 'You're proposing?'

'Not here,' he said dryly. 'I'm going to wait for more

romantic surroundings. Wash your face and then join me on the terrace and I'll do it properly.'

Her insides fluttering with excitement, Libby waited for him to go and then tried to concentrate on removing the evidence of hysterical crying.

Did Andreas truly want to marry her?

The thought of spending the rest of her life with him made her feel giddy with happiness.

How could she ever have thought that she didn't love him?

How could she have fooled herself for so long?

She adored him.

And he was about to propose to her. And she knew exactly what her answer was going to be.

Smiling, she wandered back into the bedroom and opened one of the drawers, looking for a tissue.

And then she saw the letter.

She probably wouldn't have looked twice at it if it hadn't been for the fact that the bold handwriting seemed to leap from the page and the first four words penetrated her brain like a sharpened knife.

Andreas, I love you.

Feeling suddenly sick, Libby reached down and picked up the letter, opening it up so that she could read the rest of it.

I really enjoyed this week together and I can't wait to be your wife.

Your loving Eleni.

Libby stared down at the letter for endless minutes, as if hoping that by studying the words hard enough they might alter their shape in front of her horrified eyes.

But they didn't.

They stayed the same, while the sick feeling inside her grew and grew.

Still holding the letter, she walked towards the terrace, hesitating slightly as she saw Andreas standing with his back to her, his broad shoulders blocking the view of the ocean.

He heard her approach and turned, the smile on his face fading as he saw her.

'You're as white as a sheet. What's the matter?'

She swallowed and dropped the letter on the table in front of her. 'This is the matter.'

He frowned slightly and picked up the letter, sucking in a breath as he scanned the contents. 'Libby—'

'Just don't even try and explain,' she advised him shakily, backing away from him so quickly that she stumbled into one of the chairs. She reached out a hand to steady herself and found that it was trembling.

He tensed. 'It isn't—'

'I believed you, Andreas!' She looked at him accusingly. 'When you told me that I was the only woman you'd ever loved, *I believed you*. But you're just like all the others. One woman isn't enough for you!'

Andreas swore softly and stepped towards her. 'Will you listen to me?'

'No.' Libby shook her head firmly, 'When you said that you were intending to propose, I didn't realise that there was a queue. So tell me, Andreas, when exactly did you plan to fit me in?'

'Eleni is not my wife.' His voice was terse and she tried to hide the pain she was feeling.

'Not yet maybe, but she obviously thinks that it's going to happen soon.'

Andreas gave an impatient growl and slammed his fist down on the table.

'Libby, less than half an hour ago I told you that I loved you. Do you really think I would say those words when I was planning to marry another woman?'

'Of course I do! Men do things like that all the time!' Libby's chest rose and fell as she struggled to breathe. What usually happened naturally now seemed to take considerable effort. 'Are you seriously trying to tell me that you had no relationship with her?'

He ran long fingers through his hair in an impatient gesture. 'I'm not saying that, but—'

'But you conveniently forgot to mention her,' Libby interrupted hoarsely. 'When I asked you about other women, you said that there wasn't anyone special—'

'Because there wasn't,' he said wearily, his hands dropping to his sides.

'She thinks she's going to marry you, Andreas.' Libby heard her voice wobble and hated herself for it. 'That sounds pretty special to me.'

There was a long silence and when he looked up his eyes were tired. 'For a short time I did think that I would marry her, but it's history now. On the other hand, perhaps we should both be grateful that you found that note because it's proved to both of us that you just aren't capable of trusting anyone.' His voice seemed to have lost all its warmth. 'I've told you that I love you more times than I can count, and I've shown you in as many ways as I know. If you still can't trust my feelings or your own then there's definitely no future for us. No relationship can work without trust and you just can't give it. You damn me without even listening to my side of the story.'

Libby looked at him, wondering how anyone could survive such highs and lows of emotions over such a short time. Less than an hour ago he'd been promising to make babies with her. Now their relationship appeared to be in pieces.

And he was blaming her.

In fact, he looked angrier than she'd ever imagined he could be. She was used to him being good-humoured and relaxed about everything, but he certainly wasn't relaxed now.

How could he blame her? She shook her head incredulously. 'Look at it from my point of view, Andreas. If you'd found that letter in my bedroom, what would you have done?'

'What would I have done?' His handsome face was devoid of emotion. 'I would have asked you about it, Libby, knowing that you would have had a perfectly innocent explanation. Knowing that I was the man you loved. You see, I trust you, *agape mou*.'

She looked at him in stunned silence and he shook his head slowly, his expression sad. 'I love you, Libby, and I know you love me, but it's never going to work between us unless you break down that great big wall you've built around yourself and learn to trust me, too.'

'Andreas—'

'Forget it.' His jaw tightened. 'There's a flight leaving for Heathrow late this afternoon. I'll book you on it. Our date is over, Libby.'

CHAPTER TEN

'ALL right, what happened?' Katy dragged Libby into the treatment room, her expression serious. 'It's been a whole week now and you still haven't told me anything. Even Alex is worried about you. He's ready to kill Andreas but he doesn't know what the motive is.'

Libby looked at her. 'It's just the usual.'

Katy frowned. 'What do you mean, *the usual*?'

Libby's eyes filled. 'Andreas had someone else.'

Katy stared at her for a moment and then shook her head. 'No. No way.'

'It's true.'

Katy wrinkled her nose and shook her head again. 'It can't be. Not Andreas. He loves you, Lib, I know he does.'

Libby shrugged and tried to look casual but it was impossibly hard. She felt raw inside. 'So? Since when has that stopped a man from forming other relationships?'

'You've had some rotten experiences,' Katy admitted quietly, 'and I know how badly it's affected you, but I'm sure that this time you're wrong. Andreas is crazy about you. I know he is. Tell me what happened.'

'I found a letter…' Libby found herself telling every detail of that awful afternoon while Katy listened.

'But it doesn't make sense, Lib,' her sister said finally. 'Why would he virtually propose to you if he was planning to marry another woman? There must be a simple explanation.'

'The explanation is that he's the same as every other man,' Libby said stiffly, and Katy shook her head.

'You're not thinking straight,' she said. 'I'm absolutely sure that Andreas isn't the sort of man who would have two women on the go at the same time. He's too traditional. For goodness' sake, Lib, can't you see that?'

Libby stared at her. 'What do you mean?'

Katy sighed. 'For a bright girl, you're very dense when it comes to people. He's Greek, Libby. Family is hugely important to him. You said that he'd virtually proposed to you. Why would he do that if he was in love with someone else?'

'I don't know,' Libby confessed, 'and he didn't offer any sort of explanation.'

'Knowing you, you went in with all guns blazing and didn't give the guy a chance to explain.'

Libby stiffened defensively and then her shoulders sagged. That was exactly what had happened. For the first time she wondered if she'd been too hasty. Maybe there was an innocent explanation for the letter.

'I just find it impossible to trust him,' she said miserably. 'It's me, Katy. It's all my fault. I'm so messed up I don't think I'll ever be able to trust anyone. Perhaps you'd better just shoot me.'

Katy sighed and gave her a hug. 'I'm not going to shoot you. We're busy enough in A and E as it is. And you're not messed up. You're just very wary of being hurt after everything that's happened in your life. It's the same with Alex. You're both commitment-phobes and I suppose our parents can take the blame for that really. We grew up watching a perfect example of a disastrous relationship. But you've got to put that behind you, Lib.'

Libby struggled for control. 'I don't know how.'

'Do you love him?'

Libby gave her a wobbly smile. 'Oh, yes. So much.'

Katy beamed. 'Well, that's good.'

'Is it?' Libby sniffed and rummaged in her pocket for a tissue. It certainly didn't feel good. It felt agonisingly painful and getting through each day was a mammoth exercise in willpower.

'Of course it's good. A month ago you didn't think you could ever fall in love. At least you've moved past that stage.'

'I think I preferred that stage,' Libby said miserably. 'It didn't hurt as much as this stage.'

Katy ignored her. 'All you need to do now is relax and trust him.'

'It's too late,' Libby said. 'He's already decided I'm a lost cause.'

Katy shook her head. 'You really are hopeless sometimes. You can't switch love on and off, Lib. If he loves you then he loves you. And I'm willing to bet he's suffering as much as you are.'

'He said that our relationship didn't have a future.'

'Until you learn to trust him,' Katy finished, and Libby looked at her helplessly.

'You make it sound so simple but I have absolutely no idea how to do that.' She looked at her sister. 'How do I do that?'

Katy smiled. 'You have to believe that what you share is special. That it isn't something he could possibly find with anyone else.' She paused. 'Is it special, Libby?'

Libby stared at her, remembering the way she and Andreas had connected from the first moment they'd met, the laughter they'd shared, how well they worked together—and then she remembered their incredible physical relationship.

'It's special,' she croaked finally, and Katy's smile broadened.

'Good. Admitting that is the first step to learning to trust. Why would he damage anything so special?'

'Because men do that all the time?'

Katy shook her head. 'No. I disagree. There are plenty of mediocre and bad relationships out there and it's hardly surprising that they go wrong because they were always wrong. But when a relationship is special it stays special and it doesn't go wrong, Libby. It just grows stronger. Providing you let it.'

Libby gave a wobbly smile. 'You're back to your psychiatrist mode again. Are you leaving A and E?'

Katy glanced at her watch and pulled a face. 'If I don't get back to work soon, the answer is very probably. But I'm serious, Libby. You have to acknowledge that what you have together is something that neither of you is going to throw away.'

Libby stood still, recognising the truth in her sister's words. What she and Andreas shared *was* special. 'So what do I do?'

Katy grinned. 'You go for it, angel. If you want him—and I know that you do—then don't let him get away.'

'What if he doesn't want me any more? What if it's too late?'

Katy sighed. 'You're doing it again—not trusting your relationship. Not believing in the love you have for each other. Love doesn't die overnight, Libby. Andreas still wants you, but he wants you to believe that what you share is special, too. You need to show him that you do. You need to show him that it's so special you're not going to give up on it.' She gave her sister another hug and then made for the door. 'I want to be your matron-of-honour while I still have something resembling a waistline so you'd better get a move on.'

With that she pushed open the door of the treatment room and left Libby to return to the ward, totally distracted by their conversation.

'There you are.' Bev hurried up, an expression of relief on her face. 'The SHO just called us from A and E. He's taken a call from a GP who's sending in a three-year-old with a high fever and vomiting. Can you get the side room ready?'

Libby hurried off to do as Bev requested and as an afterthought laid up a trolley for a lumbar puncture just in case it was needed.

She'd just finished the room when the little boy arrived on the ward accompanied by the paramedics who'd been called by the GP.

'This is Max King,' one of the paramedics told her. 'He's been ill since last night but he's gone downhill very fast.'

Jonathon, the SHO, was by his side and looked distinctly flustered. 'I've been calling Andreas, but I'm not getting an answer,' he muttered to Libby. She sensed immediately that he was out of his depth and one glance at the child confirmed the reason.

The little boy was drowsy and irritable and his breathing was rapid. One touch of his dry, scorching skin confirmed that his temperature was sky-high.

'All right, Max,' she soothed gently, 'we'll soon have you sorted out.'

'I'll try bleeping Andreas again,' the SHO muttered, and Libby caught his arm as he went to leave the room.

'Has the child had penicillin yet?' she asked urgently, lowering her voice so that the parents didn't hear her question him.

The SHO shook his head and glanced at the little boy. 'I was waiting for Andreas to look at him. There's no rash or anything, so I didn't think—'

'Get some penicillin inside him now,' Libby ordered softly, knowing that the doctor was still relatively inexperienced and not wanting to take any chances. 'There doesn't have to be a rash for it to be meningitis and that child is very sick. Do it, and then we can do the rest of the investigations knowing that at least we've covered that option. He's showing definite signs of raised intracranial pressure.'

She'd nursed children with meningitis before and she knew that the presentation often varied. But it was still a lethal disease and she wasn't taking any chances while they waited for Andreas.

Jonathon hesitated and then nodded. 'All right. If you think so.'

'I do,' Libby said firmly, reaching for the penicillin that she'd put on the trolley. She turned to the parents, her tone calm and reassuring. 'We're just going to give him some antibiotics. Do you know his weight?'

She calculated the dose based on what the parents told her and then handed it to Jonathon, who checked it and gave it to the restless child.

Max's mother, Heather, was white with anxiety. 'You think it might be meningitis, don't you?'

'It's a possibility,' Libby said gently, 'which is why we've given the penicillin at the earliest time, but our consultant will be here soon and—'

'I'm here.'

Libby felt a rush of relief as she recognised the voice behind her. She'd never been so pleased to see Andreas in her life.

'This is Dr Christakos.' She introduced him to the parents, realising just how much she loved him. Just how much faith she had in him.

Andreas was by the child's side in an instant, taking the handover from Jonathon as he examined the sick little boy.

'You poor little thing,' he murmured gently, his large hands gently palpating the child's abdomen. 'Jonathon, has he had penicillin?'

'Yes.' The SHO shot Libby a look of gratitude. 'Libby thought we should go ahead with that and not wait for you.'

'Good decision.'

Andreas completed his examination and straightened. 'I want to do a lumbar puncture straight away—can you lay up a trolley?'

'It's here.' Libby pushed it forward and a small smile played around his firm mouth.

'Do you ever get anything wrong?'

Her heart beat slightly faster. 'Yes. But when I do, I try to put it right.'

For a brief moment his dark eyes were questioning and then he strode over to the sink and started scrubbing, talking to the parents as he prepared to perform the lumbar puncture.

He explained what he was planning to do and why, and Heather clung to her husband, the worry visible on her face.

'Perhaps you would rather wait outside while we do this,' Andreas suggested, but Heather shook her head.

'No. I don't want to leave him.'

Andreas looked at Libby. 'We'll do it in the treatment room. I want to get a line in first but then someone needs to hold him for the LP.'

'I'll hold him,' she said immediately, 'and I'll ask Bev to find someone to assist you.'

Moments later they were all gathered in the treatment room and Andreas inserted a line with ease. That done, Libby gently turned Max on his side, talking quietly to him all the time.

She curved the little boy round so that his knees were up by his chin, flexing the spine, and watched while Andreas marked the skin with a pen and then draped and sterilised the area.

Bev settled Heather at the head of the trolley. 'Sit there and talk to him,' she suggested quietly, 'but keep your back to Dr Christakos and then you won't have to watch what's happening.'

Andreas infiltrated the skin with local anaesthetic and then tested the site, his eyes flickering to hers.

'Are you ready?' She nodded and held Max firmly, knowing how crucial it was that the child didn't move during the procedure.

She watched as Andreas inserted the LP needle, talking quietly to the child and occasionally making a comment to Jonathon who was watching.

Bev had three little bottles ready and Andreas let four drops of fluid fall into each bottle.

Once Andreas was satisfied, he withdrew the needle and cleaned the site before covering it with the dressing that Bev had ready.

'All done.' He pushed his chair away from the side of the trolley and stood up, ripping off his gloves and dropping them in the nearest bin. 'We'll get those samples to the lab urgently and in the meantime we'll get a line in and start getting fluids into the little chap.'

Max had stopped wailing now and was lying on the trolley, moaning quietly.

Andreas turned to his SHO with a list of instructions and tests that he wanted performed. He was leaving absolutely nothing to chance.

'Let's get him back to the room and let him sleep,' he said quietly, his gaze flickering to the parents. 'I'm sorry. This is all very worrying for you, I know, and I'm aware that we haven't had much time for explanations because of the urgency of the situation. If there is anything you'd like to ask me now, please do so.'

Heather's eyes filled. 'He looks so poorly. What will happen?'

'We wait for the results of these tests and we watch him,' Andreas said, his eyes flickering to the child who was shifting restlessly on the trolley. He frowned slightly and pulled back the sheet Libby had used to cover Max. 'He has a rash.'

Libby followed his gaze and saw that the child had indeed developed a rash all over his body.

Andreas looked at her and his eyes were warm. 'You did the right thing, giving that penicillin,' he said softly, and she swallowed.

She really needed to talk to him but she didn't know when an opportunity was going to present itself.

*   *   *

Max started to improve over the next two days and once it was clear that he was no longer on the critical list, his parents started to relax slightly and even take short breaks away from the room.

Andreas had maintained a constant presence on the ward when the child had first been admitted, but once Max was out of danger he'd visited less frequently, kept busy by the other considerable demands of his job.

He made no attempt to seek Libby out and she wondered if it was intentional.

Was he giving her space?

Did he realise that she was desperate to speak to him?

In the end she came up with a plan and waited nervously for him to appear on the ward.

It was almost the end of her shift when he finally arrived, looking grim-faced after dealing with a tough case in A and E.

'I wanted to check on Max before I went home,' he said, walking past her into the room and smiling at the little boy.

'Well, someone's looking better,' he murmured, watching as Max played happily with some toy cars that Libby had found for him in the playroom. 'He is one lucky boy.'

Libby nodded, watching while he checked him over. 'I wonder why the GP didn't give penicillin?'

Andreas straightened. 'Who knows? But the sooner your brother Alex gets out there the better, if you ask me.'

Libby smiled. 'Alex won't be working in London. He's found himself a practice in Cornwall so that he can sail and windsurf and indulge in all the other hobbies he loves.'

Andreas looked at her. 'What will you do about the flat?'

She blushed slightly. 'I don't know yet. His job doesn't start until the end of August.' She took a deep breath. 'Andreas, I wanted to give you something.'

She reached into her pocket and pulled out the envelope she'd been carrying with her all week.

He took it with a frown and was about to open it when

Bev stuck her head round the door and announced that he was wanted in A and E urgently.

'Again?' Andreas rolled his eyes and pocketed the envelope. 'I'll see you later. Maybe.' His dark eyes were weary. 'Unless it turns out to be a long one.'

It was a long one and Libby was at home, making herself a hot chocolate in her oldest jeans and a skimpy pink strap top, when the doorbell rang.

Libby opened the door, her heart pounding when she saw Andreas standing there.

He waved the envelope in her face, his expression wary. 'You gave me a cheque for £1000.'

She nodded and stood to one side so that he could come in, but he didn't move.

Instead, he frowned ominously. 'You don't owe me any money. I paid for a date and that's what we had, Libby.'

'And now it's my turn,' she croaked, wishing that she was wearing heels. She was standing in bare feet and he towered above her. 'I want a date, Andreas, and £1000 seems to be the going rate. A bit steep, but I happen to think you're worth it.'

There was a long silence and then he finally stepped inside her flat and closed the door firmly behind him.

'What are you saying?' His Greek accent was suddenly very pronounced and she fiddled with the hem of her top nervously, wondering whether he was going to walk away once she'd said what she had to say.

'I want a date, Andreas, and as you're obviously not going to ask me again, I thought I'd better ask you.'

'Why do you want a date?' His voice was hoarse and she took a deep breath, wondering why they were having this conversation in the hallway.

'Because I want to be with you,' she said simply. 'And the reason I want to be with you is because I love you. And I know that what we have is too special to throw away.'

He closed his eyes briefly. 'I never thought I'd hear you say that.'

'And I never thought I'd say it,' Libby admitted. 'But then I met you and you changed the way I felt about everything.'

Andreas was very still. 'I thought you didn't trust me.'

'I was wrong. I do trust you. And I'm sorry I overreacted about that letter. It was just that everything between us was so new—so special—I just couldn't believe that it wouldn't go wrong.'

He still didn't make a move towards her. 'Don't you want to know about Eleni?'

Libby shook her head. 'All I need to know is that you love me,' she said softly. 'That's all that matters.'

He gave a groan and hauled her into his arms. 'I love you but I'd given up hoping that you'd ever believe me.'

Libby buried her face in his chest. 'I know. I'm sorry. I'm a hopeless case. The truth is I've never been in love before, and when it finally happened it all seemed too good to be true.'

He slid his hands round her face and forced her to look at him. 'I was at fault, too. I underestimated just how hard it is for you to trust people. You've built this huge wall around yourself.'

'It seemed the only way to survive.'

He stroked her cheek gently. 'Tell me about your parents. I want to understand why you feel the way you do,' he said quietly. 'You hardly ever talk about them.'

Libby pulled a face. 'That's because they're not my favourite topic of conversation.' She took a deep breath and pulled away from him slightly. 'Let's just say that when I was growing up they weren't like everyone else's parents. Alex always says that the only reason the three of us have turned out remotely normal is because they had the sense to send us to boarding school.'

Andreas frowned. 'It was that bad?'

'Worse. For the first twenty-eight years of my life there was absolutely no evidence that my parents loved each other,' Libby said bitterly. 'They argued, Dad drank too much, and when he drank...' She broke off and Andreas looked at her.

'What happened when he drank? Was he violent?'

'Sometimes.' Libby rubbed her fingers across her forehead. 'I suspect it was more than sometimes but we were at school so we didn't really see it. It only happened once when we were at home and Alex went for him with a cricket bat. I called the police and I don't think Dad ever really forgave me for that. But it wasn't just the violence. It was the fact that they showed no affection towards each other and Dad had one affair after another.'

'But they're still together?'

'Amazingly, yes.' Libby gave a wry smile. 'Years ago Dad ruined Katy's relationship with Jago because he didn't approve, and when they met up again years later Mum was so furious about what he'd done that she stood up to him for the first time in her life. I think the prospect of losing her brought him to his senses.'

'Well, in the circumstances it's hardly surprising that you don't think relationships can work.'

'It wasn't just Mum and Dad,' Libby confessed. 'Apart from Jago, all the men I meet seem to be utterly faithless and without morals. Even Alex, who I adore, is a real bastard to women.'

'And Philip?'

Libby laughed. 'I was never serious about Philip, but all the same it was a real blow to my ego. I only ever seem to be everyone's second choice. That's why I couldn't quite believe what was happening between us. It was too good to be true.'

Andreas nodded. 'I understand now why you were so upset about the letter you found. Your confidence was so fragile that you couldn't risk trusting me.'

'That's true.' Libby flushed and bit her lip. 'And it's also true that you're so gorgeous and eligible I just couldn't understand what you were doing with me, apart from amusing yourself.'

'Would you like me to spell it out?' Andreas smiled and then gave a sigh. 'I'm going to tell you about Eleni, Libby, if only to prove to you just how much I love you.'

'There's no need—'

'I want to,' he said firmly. 'I met Eleni when I worked in Boston. She's a lawyer and we knew each other vaguely from functions in Athens that we'd both attended. We started dating, I suppose because we were both Greek as much as anything else.'

'And you were in love with her?'

'No. And that was the problem.' He gave a wry smile. 'She was desperate to get married. At the time I thought she loved me but I think the truth was probably that she just wanted to achieve the degree of respectability that marriage gives you if you're Greek. She was thirty-two and that's old to still be single in our culture. She saw me as a useful way out of her predicament. That was when she wrote me the letter. I didn't know it was still in the drawer. I hadn't been to the villa for six months.'

'So what happened?'

Andreas pulled a face. 'Adrienne was what happened. My mother was becoming concerned that I might marry Eleni and she knew that she was totally unsuitable for me. So she suddenly decided that Adrienne should live with me.'

'But how did that effect your relationship with Eleni?'

'The minute Eleni knew that I had responsibility for Adrienne she lost interest in me,' he said dryly. 'Eleni is not remotely maternal and the thought of being saddled with a moody teenager quickly destroyed any plans she might have had about marrying me. And also my mother knew I'd never marry a career-woman.'

Libby rolled her eyes. 'I'm in love with a raving chauvinist.'

He grinned. 'I'm Greek, *agape mou*, and Greek men are very traditional. I want a woman who's happy to raise children with me.'

Libby raised an eyebrow. 'Barefoot and pregnant?'

He glanced under the table to her bare feet. 'I actually quite like those ridiculous heels you favour, but I love your bare feet, too. In fact, I love everything about you. The moment I saw you buried under a pile of children I knew you were the woman I wanted to marry.'

'I thought you wanted me because I presented a challenge,' Libby admitted, and he smiled.

'I wanted you because I fell madly in love for the first time in my life. So what do you say, Libby? Are you prepared to marry a very traditional Greek male?'

'Yes. And just to prove it, there's a surprise waiting for you in my kitchen.'

Andreas lifted an eyebrow and glanced towards the closed door. 'A surprise?'

Libby shrugged. 'Why don't you go and find out?'

Andreas pushed open the kitchen door and then smiled with delight. 'Adrienne? What are you doing here?'

His niece flung her arms around his neck and hugged him tightly. 'Libby collected me earlier. She said that I don't have to board any more. She told me that you've finally found a perfect housekeeper.'

Andreas cast a questioning look at Libby and she blushed.

'I thought, between the two of us, we ought to be able to manage our shifts so that one of us can pick her up from school.'

Andreas smiled and held out a hand to her. 'So I take it that your answer is yes? I thought you didn't believe in happy endings.'

She walked up to him and slid her arms around both of them. 'I didn't until I met you, and the answer is definitely yes. As we're going to get married, do you think *Yiayia* will mind if I kiss you in front of Adrienne?'

Without waiting for an answer, she stood on tiptoe and gave him a lingering kiss on the lips.

Adrienne gave a squeal of excitement. 'You're really going to get married? Can I be a bridesmaid?'

There was a brief pause while Libby reluctantly disengaged herself. 'Absolutely! Which means that we girls have got some serious shopping to do.'

Andreas groaned. 'Just don't take me near that hairdresser again.'

Libby's eyes twinkled. 'Afraid you might be tempted?'

Andreas pulled her against him. 'There's only ever going to be one person who tempts me, *agape mou*—remember that.'

Libby lifted her mouth for his kiss. 'I will.'

EPILOGUE

THE reception was in full swing and Libby relaxed back in her chair, smiling as she watched people enjoying the dancing.

'Stop looking so happy.' Alex pulled out the chair next to her and sat down, stretching his long legs out in front of him. 'I suppose it was all the chocolate you put on the menu.'

Libby laughed. 'Did you enjoy it?'

'Apart from the chocolate-coated prawns,' Alex said dryly, helping himself to her glass of champagne. 'They challenged my palate. Where's Andreas?'

'Talking to Katy. She's trying to persuade him to tell her where we're going on our honeymoon.'

'He still hasn't told you?'

'No. It's a surprise.' Libby sighed dreamily. 'Isn't it romantic?'

'Not really.' Alex took a large slug of champagne. 'The guy probably just hasn't made up his mind yet. Don't read anything into it.'

Libby smiled placidly. 'Today I'm too happy to hit anyone. Even you. How's your date?'

Alex's gaze flickered across the room and rested on a curvaceous blonde who was laughing loudly with a group of guests.

'A bit like your chocolate. Better in small quantities.'

'Your problem is that you're dating the wrong women,' Libby said sagely, and he gave a wicked grin.

'I know. It's something that I work *really* hard at.'

Libby reached across and took his hand. 'I want you to be happy, Alex.'

He frowned at her. 'Are you drunk?'

She looked pointedly at the glass of champagne in his hand. 'How can *I* be drunk when *you're* drinking my champagne?'

'Then what's all this sentimental nonsense about me being happy?' He cast her a bored look. 'I'm happy.'

Libby shook her head. 'No, I mean I want you to be settled down with children.'

Alex lifted an eyebrow mockingly. 'I thought you said you wanted me to be happy.'

Libby sighed. 'Don't you ever want children of your own?'

Alex shook his head, his blue eyes suddenly cool. 'No. I do not.'

'You'd be a great father.'

Her brother's broad shoulders tensed and all traces of humour vanished from his handsome face. 'We both know that's not true.'

'Somewhere out there, there's a woman for you,' Libby said firmly, and Alex drained the champagne glass.

'Well, hopefully if I keep my head down she won't see me.' He put the glass down on the table, his blue eyes glittering. 'I don't do commitment, Libby. You know that.'

'I didn't think I did either,' Libby said, 'and look at me now.'

'I'm looking,' Alex drawled, a hint of a smile touching his hard mouth. 'And so are most of the male guests. You're the only bride I've ever met who thinks that ''something blue'' refers to the length of your dress. Were they short of fabric?'

Libby laughed. 'I didn't want to go down the aisle looking like a blancmange. Not my style. And anyway a long dress would have hidden my shoes. Don't you just *love* my shoes?'

Alex glanced down. 'I think the SAS use something similar for weapons training.'

Still laughing, Libby leaned across and kissed him. 'You're a total pain but surprisingly enough I'm going to miss you. Why do you have to go to Cornwall? Why can't you be a GP in London?'

Alex was suddenly still. 'Actually, I'm not going to be a GP,' he said casually. 'I miss the pace of A and E.'

Her eyes widened. 'You're going back to trauma?'

'I am.'

'Where?'

'In Cornwall. I need a change of scenery.' Alex gave a wicked smile. 'And, anyway, I've been out with all the blonde women in London.'

Libby looked at him thoughtfully. 'Perhaps that's where you're going wrong. Perhaps you should pick a woman who isn't blonde. What you need is a tiny, dark-haired girl with a flat chest.'

Alex threw back his head and laughed, and Libby caught her breath. Her brother was astonishingly handsome. It was hardly surprising that he broke hearts everywhere he went.

He was still smiling as he looked at her. 'Why on earth would I need someone like that?'

'Because all the women you've dated so far have failed to keep your attention for longer than five minutes,' Libby explained with impeccable logic, 'so you need to date someone who is totally opposite to your usual.'

'Thanks for the advice,' Alex said dryly, standing up and nodding briefly as Andreas approached. 'Are you absolutely sure you did the right thing, marrying this woman? I mean, according to Adrienne, women were queuing up to marry you.'

'I did the right thing.' Andreas held out a hand and gave a slow smile that made Libby's heart race. Suddenly she forgot about her brother. All she could think about was her own future, with the man she loved.

She stood up and held out a hand. 'Time to smash some plates, Dr Christakos.'

And Andreas led her onto the dance-floor.

REQUEST YOUR
FREE BOOKS!

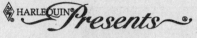

2 FREE NOVELS
PLUS 2
FREE GIFTS!

YES! Please send me 2 FREE Harlequin Presents® novels and my 2 FREE gifts. After receiving them, if I don't wish to receive any more books, I can return the shipping statement marked "cancel." If I don't cancel, I will receive 6 brand-new novels every month and be billed just $3.80 per book in the U.S., or $4.47 per book in Canada, plus 25¢ shipping and handling per book and applicable taxes, if any*. That's a savings of close to 15% off the cover price! I understand that accepting the 2 free books and gifts places me under no obligation to buy anything. I can always return a shipment and cancel at any time. Even if I never buy another book from Harlequin, the two free books and gifts are mine to keep forever.

106 HDN EEXK 306 HDN EEXV

Name _____ (PLEASE PRINT) _____

Address _____ Apt. # _____

City _____ State/Prov. _____ Zip/Postal Code _____

Signature (if under 18, a parent or guardian must sign) _____

Mail to the **Harlequin Reader Service®**:
IN U.S.A.: P.O. Box 1867, Buffalo, NY 14240-1867
IN CANADA: P.O. Box 609, Fort Erie, Ontario L2A 5X3

Not valid to current Harlequin Presents subscribers.

Want to try two free books from another line?
Call 1-800-873-8635 or visit www.morefreebooks.com.

* Terms and prices subject to change without notice. NY residents add applicable sales tax. Canadian residents will be charged applicable provincial taxes and GST. This offer is limited to one order per household. All orders subject to approval. Credit or debit balances in a customer's account(s) may be offset by any other outstanding balance owed by or to the customer. Please allow 4 to 6 weeks for delivery.

Your Privacy: Harlequin is committed to protecting your privacy. Our Privacy Policy is available online at www.eHarlequin.com or upon request from the Reader Service. From time to time we make our lists of customers available to reputable firms who may have a product or service of interest to you. If you would prefer we not share your name and address, please check here. ☐

HP07

HARLEQUIN *Presents*

Passion and Seduction Guaranteed!

She's sexy, successful and pregnant!

Relax and enjoy our fabulous series about couples whose passion results in pregnancies… sometimes unexpected!

Share the surprises, emotions, drama and suspense as our parents-to-be come to terms with the prospect of bringing a new life into the world. All will discover that the business of making babies brings with it the most special joy of all.…

February's Arrival:

PREGNANT BY THE MILLIONAIRE
by Carole Mortimer

What happens when Hebe Johnson finds out she's pregnant with her noncommittal boss's baby?

Find out when you buy your copy of this title today!